LOCAL PRAISE FOR

Swing Bridge

"Loved it! Bronwyn hits a home run with her debut work "Swing Bridge," a short story collection that will make you laugh, cry and think. Well done!"
—**William E. Johnson**, Award-winning Author
of *A Silent Tide* and *A Silent Siege*

"Loosen your seatbelt, open a beer, and bounce down a dusty dirt road in the country where old school values collide with the contemporary world."
—**Ned & Dia Lawless**, Pizza Entrepreneurs

"Swing Bridge captures life in Tidewater Virginia through unforgettable characters! From Fig Girl (my favorite) to Pocahontas and the Judys. This collection is a read that will stay with you, stories well-worth reading again and again."
—**bobbi hatton**, President of the
Mathews County Visitor & Information Center

"Quirky, enjoyable, relatable and relevant. Swing Bridge captures the tensions, inspirations and personalities of small town life on the Chesapeake as only someone who has lived here would know."
—**Greg & Lori Dusenberry**, The Inn at Tabbs Creek

"This rich collection closely reflects rural communities whatever the location. Moving from one story to the next, the reader immediately identifies with the characters, whether it be the Fig-Girl or the heroic EMT staff member faced with a difficult decision. I enjoyed these stories immensely!"
—**Bette Dillehay**, Director of the Mathews Memorial Library

"Bronwyn's ability to intertwine memorable characters with local landmarks and events into engaging stories is truly noteworthy! Kudos!"
—**Jan Towne**, Mathews Blueways Water Trails

"Interesting stories! I've lived here all my life, retired from working on a tugboat 22 years ago. The characters in Swing Bridge feel real, like I recognize them from around town."

—**Ben Richardson**, Put-in Creek Carvings on Main Street

"These stories are the perfect way to laze away an afternoon, nosing around and seeing what the neighbors are 'gittin' up to."

—**Missy Whaley**, Middlesex High School Librarian

"A time capsule for small-town America with all its comforts and thorny problems. Such a good read!"

—**Christine Johnson**, Director of the Mathews Outdoor Club

"These stories are an invitation to introspection, an opportunity to examine your own biases, prejudices, and values through the actions of Bronwyn's characters and the histories she presents. The tales are wrapped in the unique culture of rural Tidewater, Virginia, with its scars and harsh truths presented in a clear, yet sympathetic light. For the come-heres who live in this borrowed landscape, the stories offer a deeper understanding of the people who have called these water and roadways home for generations, as well as enlightening us to the judgment we may be unwittingly bringing to bear. Issues of morality, property rights, personal awakening, prejudice, compassion, loyalty, ethics, the complicated bonds of family, deceit, racism, loss, bodily autonomy, and the parallel truths of history and self are examined by characters who are impressively developed in a few short pages. These stories are for reading, and re-reading, for the discovery of new truths each time."

—**Pamela Doss**, Executive Director,
Bay School Community Arts Center

"These delightful and unusual stories explore, invert, then discard and reinvent ideas of outsiders and insiders. If the collection were a bag of potato chips, they would be Old Bay flavored. Could you want anything more, honestly?"

—**Karen Holmberg**, Volcanologist

The following stories have been previously published: "Fig-Girl" in *The Atherton Review*; "Diablo" in *Evening Street Review*; "Poplar Grove" in *SORTES Magazine*; "Dragon Run" in *Hawaii Pacific Review*; "Rescue Squad" in *Clackamas Literary Review*; "Sail Forth" in *The Quiet Reader*; "The Bel-Mar Blade" in *Isele Magazine*; "Hurricane Hole" in *Faultline Journal of Arts & Letters*; "The Kittiwake" in *Sinister Wisdom*.

Swing Bridge

Stories from Tidewater Virginia

BRONWYN HUGHES

With illustrations by
Kat Sharp

Port Haywood Press
Virginia

Port Haywood Press

ISBN 979-8-218-17253-4

Cover design by Bizhan Khodabandeh
Cover photograph by John Kenny. Website: www.johnkennyphotos.com
    Email: porchofgeese@duck.com
Interior design: Creative Publishing Book Design

In memory of Whoopi's beach house where the scavenger hunt began.

Table of Contents

Chesa
Cherry Pt.
Cemetery
Judys Toilets
This Way to
Dragon Run
Whitman's Marina
WYNN'S I.S.
Post Office
Swing Bridge
Rescue Squad
High School
Welcome to:
MOBJACK

peake Bay

Campground

Yacht Club

Poplar Grove

Trash & Treasure

Slacktide Cafe   Mosaic Mural   Library

Lucky's Diner

Truly You
Cuts 'n' Curls

Village Green

Dump

This Way to
Werowocomoco

I do not weep at the world.
I am too busy sharpening my oyster knife.

Zora Neale Hurston

Fig-Girl

THE SCREEN DOOR STRETCHED WIDE, then slammed. I dropped my bouquet of hand-picked hydrangeas next to my husband's new headstone, reassuring him I'd be right back. His grave lay next to a plot designated for me in the family cemetery, overlooking the creek.

"You're leaving *already*?" I sputtered from across the lawn. My son, Danny, was carrying his bag to his rental car. "But you just got here."

This was Danny's first visit to Wynn's Island since his father's funeral, last fall. Now that his divorce was final, I hoped he would have more time to spend with me. Couldn't he stay a few more days to help with some chores his father used to do? Scoop the pine tags from the gutters at least? I had planned crab cakes for lunch. But he said he had to get back to civilization—shorthand for highspeed internet and more bars for his cellphone.

Danny placed his paws on my old—but sturdy—shoulders. "Mom, like we discussed last night, you *have* to sell this place, and you need to sell Dad's boat. It's too much for you to manage all of this on your own." His gesture encompassed the farmhouse I was born in, built in 1860 on ten acres known as the Old Cherry Point Place, located on the windward side of Wynn's Island. The house rested on a point of land jutting into the Chesapeake Bay, wrapped on both sides by tidal creeks.

His eyes looked watery, and he had gained weight from his sitdown tech job. "Have you had a cardiac stress test recently? You look so tired and bloated. As your mother and as a nurse, I'm concerned about you."

Danny flung his bag in the trunk. He knew I didn't want to move from the Old Cherry Point Place. At eighteen, his father and I left the Island for the city of Richmond to spend the next fifty years working and raising Danny. We always planned to return, but we never expected Dan would end up in the family cemetery so soon.

"Look at all the room in your car. Are you sure you won't take any of your father's suits? His tuxedo at least? I hate to give away his good clothes." I was repeating myself. Danny had said the tech world didn't wear clothes like his father's, and besides, he didn't have any extra closet space in his Manhattan condo. He didn't even want his father's gold watch—said it would attract muggers. I offered him power tools from Dan's woodshop, his collection of opera CDs, trophies from sailing regattas. All Danny wanted was Dan's CPAP machine, electric razor and the unopened craft beer kit Danny himself had given Dan for Christmas two years ago.

"Try to sell his stuff at Tidewater Trash and Treasure," Danny suggested. "You might even be able to sell his boat through their website."

"That junk shop in town? Listen, I'll sell his boat at the marina, but I'm not selling the Old Cherry Point Place. I don't want to live in a suffocating apartment where I can't swim from my beach, or watch the moon rise over the Bay."

"Please be reasonable Mom."

"Besides, I won't be *alone*. I'm going to find live-in help—a nice lady to stay in the barn loft apartment."

"Mom, I gotta go. You should get to work on down-sizing."

Danny patted the top of my short gray bob, squeezed himself into his compact rental, and slammed the door on his seatbelt. Lowering the window, he chuckled, "Really Mom—do you even own a swimsuit?"

He programmed the GPS on his phone for West 79th Street and hollered, "LOVE YOU" into the rearview mirror as he drove over my liriope.

* * *

After Danny's visit, loneliness settled back into my joints like arthritis. Dan had died nine months ago on a beautiful fall day. Every Saturday, weather-permitting, he would set out on his fifty-foot sailboat down Stutts Creek, through Hole in the Wall, and back again to meet me for lunch at the marina. I would arrive early to drink a Bloody Mary on the porch and watch him sail back up the Creek. But that day, I spied the *Dan-Sally* returning under power with sails down. I hurried to the dock, wondering what boat system had failed and how much it would cost. A member of the Coast Guard met me. Dan had radioed for help just before suffering a fatal heart attack.

Swing Bridge

Now that I knew Danny didn't want any of his father's belongings, I felt ready to give them away. I decided to drop his suits, one each day, at the Post Office in town. We had an informal system on the Island of leaving things for people in need, a custom that began during the Depression when the only transportation to the mainland was by hand-pulled ferry. In 1939—the year I was born—we got a swing bridge, which changed everything. We lost a lot of shops that couldn't compete with businesses on the mainland, but construction work grew as come-here vacationers created a demand for big houses on the water. Through it all, the from-here tradition of leaving things anonymously at the Post Office survived.

The first suit I selected was Dan's green one with the elbow pads that he wore on St Patrick's day. I pushed open the wooden door to the Wynn Post Office and hung it over the arm of the brass light fixture. Lifting the plastic cover to kiss the lapel, I breathed in his lingering scent one last time.

The next day, when I returned with Dan's black suit that he wore to funerals, I found a bag of figs with a note stapled to it:

To the person that left me a green suit: I hope you enjoy these figs as my thanks.

Thrilled to think of a young man so proud to own that suit—and one polite enough to leave a thank you gift—I dashed home, excited to share the news with Dan. With each suit, I received another bag of figs until I was happily drowning in them. This little game gave me something to look forward to each day.

As my spirits improved, I got up my nerve to push-pin the corners of an ad onto the bulletin board at the Post Office:

Fig-Girl

Widow seeks female live-in companion to help with yardwork and chores at the Old Cherry Point Place. Will pay $300/month plus free rent in furnished barn loft apartment. One day off a week.

That was how I met the fig-giver in person.

*   *   *

Removing a tray of fig tarts from the oven, I spied a purple pickup trundling down my lane, right on time. The young woman who answered my ad deserved an "A" for punctuality. I intended to find someone older since, more than anything, I needed a companion. But after a week, nobody else had called. By the time her interview rolled around, I had talked myself into the idea of having a young person in my life, someone I could mentor.

The worn brakes of the pickup squeaked to a gentle stop behind the house. A subdued girl with straight brown hair in a neat ponytail stepped out wearing an expensive men's dress jacket, her movements soft and restrained. My teeth parted and my lips drew back, like I was in the dentist chair. *Is that girl wearing Dan's white linen blazer?*

The picture was coming clear—the figs gave it away. I peered through the dining room window. The young woman checked on her baskets of figs and fig plants in the bed of the truck, adjusting each with care. *This girl took all of Dan's suits, jackets, dress shirts and ties?* I had imagined a handsome young man, grateful for a wardrobe of dress clothes worth thousands of dollars.

When the girl turned toward the house, I rolled away from the window, wrapping myself into the drapes, wishing I could pretend not to be home. After closing my eyes for a moment, I fixed my hair and composed my facial expression as she rapped the heavy,

5

lighthouse-shaped door knocker a second time, setting off my old, blind spaniel, Millie.

"Hello ma'am. I'm Doris—I called about your ad?" She handed me *another* bag of figs. "Everyone calls me Fig-Girl." As I took the familiar bag, I realized she had no way of knowing I was the source of the suits, so I projected a grateful smile.

"What a handsome sports coat you have there. Won't you come in?" I ushered Doris into the sunroom with a grand view of the Chesapeake Bay and gestured for her to sit in a wicker chair. Millie was still barking from her bed in the kitchen, so I hollered over my shoulder for her to be quiet. "Can I offer you something to drink? Sweet tea?"

"No thank you, ma'am. I just had a lemonade after sellin' my figs outside the Post Office. You mighta seen me there—I'm at it every mornin'."

"Actually, *I* just baked some fig tarts. Would you like one?" To Doris, this must have seemed like a bizarre coincidence. *Perfect*, I mused, *She's going to bring Dan's suits back into this house and I'm going to feed her figs back to her.*

"No thank you, ma'am. I'm vegan."

Now I was truly confused. "Doesn't vegan mean you don't eat animals or animal products?"

"Yep," Doris' face lit up. "Believe it or not, figs are fulla wasp bodies. Fact is, Adam and Eve woulda been the only ones to eat figs with no dead wasps in 'em. Now all fig trees require dead wasps for pollinatin' purposes."

I started to caution her about referencing biblical stories as historical fact, but she continued.

"It so happens, the girl fig-wasps can only lay eggs in male figs. The boy fig-wasps got two jobs: to mate with their very own sisters, then dig a tunnel through the fig to let the girls out."

I opened my mouth to change the subject, but she was in full lecture mode.

"Once they're out, girl fig-wasps carry pollen to female figs cuz, come time to lay eggs, they can't tell a male fig from a female fig. Girl wasps end up in the wrong fig half the time, and that's how the unlucky ones pass away inside female figs. They ain't dyin' in vain though, cuz that's how mother nature gets figs pollinated."

My lips drew back again in a pained smile, exposing my gums and dental work.

"Oh no, you look worried, ma'am. Don't fret about your tarts. That crunchiness? Mostly seeds. They got just a small helpin' of wasp bodies mixed in."

If my loneliness hadn't been so acute, or if I had anyone else to interview, I might not have handed this *Fig-Girl* the keys to the barn loft apartment. I comforted myself with the thought that we shared a love of science.

* * *

The morning after Doris moved in, she rose before dawn to skinny dip in the Bay. Millie sensed her presence and barked from her bed in the kitchen until I emerged from my bedroom wearing a bathrobe and slippers. I didn't know why Millie was barking until the sun lit the horizon. The water and sky were ablaze with pinks and blues, silhouetting Doris' figure bobbing nude in the water.

Dan was a morning person too. After he died, I slid back into my pattern of staying up late reading, but I regretted missing those

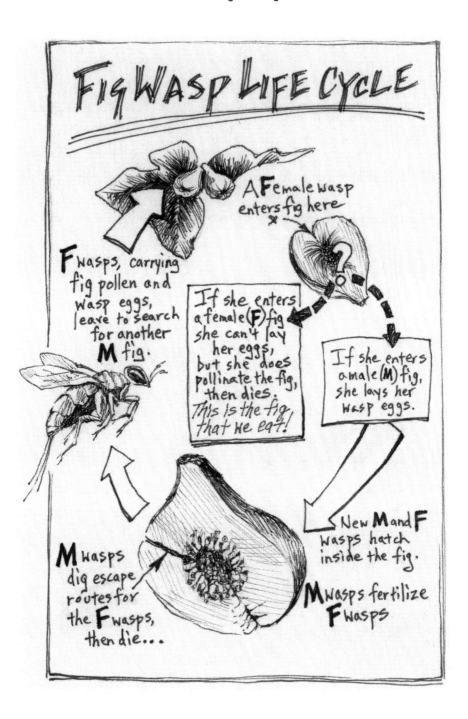

sunrises, no two ever the same. Dan used to crank his opera arias at the moment when the sun breached the horizon, my cue to come out and make him a poached egg and a slice of toast.

Not quite awake, I started to make an egg for Doris, out of habit. I watched her come out of the water and flop on the beach. After a while, she began to hunt for things in the sand, washing her findings in the surf. I couldn't help but notice what a nice figure this strange girl had. *How old was she? Early twenties? Why did she wear boxy men's clothing that hid her beautiful shape?* Her breasts were round and full, like a fresh pair of figs.

When Doris gathered her treasure to return to the apartment over the garage, I ducked from the window because she was walking up the lawn completely nude. Snapping off the stove (I couldn't offer her an egg like *that*), I rinsed the stubborn yolk down the drain, remembering Doris was vegan anyway.

Doris never missed a morning selling her figs outside the Post Office—my chance to snoop in her room. She had almost no belongings, besides Dan's suits of course. Her other possessions fit into two shoe boxes. I opened the first, afraid I would find drugs or worse, but instead it contained the most impressive collection of arrowheads I had ever seen. I ran my index finger across the sharp edge of one, thumbing the scalloped stone. The other box contained neat stacks of twenty-dollar bills wrapped with rubber-bands. In a small notebook, she had recorded her fig earnings each week, going back four years. Savings of close to nine thousand dollars. *What was she saving for? A new truck?*

Despite Doris' habit of wearing Dan's suits every day (*wrinkled*, with the sleeves *rolled up!*), I had chanced upon an amiable companion. After she returned from managing her fig business, we would spend the rest of the day running errands, doing yard work, and cooking meals together. As I suspected, Doris' education ended with high school. I enjoyed introducing her to the arts and the world of ideas. My first order of business was to correct her appalling grammar. She seemed grateful for the attention and made rapid progress. After washing and drying the dinner dishes each night, we would live-stream an opera from the Met, or watch something on PBS, or the History Channel. She seemed happy to absorb whatever I suggested.

One day, as I was showing her Dan's sailing trophies, Doris said, "Mrs. T?" That's what she called me, even though I encouraged her to call me Sally. "What kind of nurse were you?" She was holding up a life-sized silicone breast the hospital staff had all signed at my retirement party.

"I worked in a breast cancer treatment center in Richmond for forty years."

Eyes wide, she peppered me with questions about nursing, showing great interest in such things as how to care for a patient after a mastectomy. She even asked to borrow my out-of-date textbooks, returning each day with more questions.

After a couple of months, her unwavering interest in my career gave me an idea: I would pay for her to take an introductory nursing class at the local community college.

The one-year anniversary of Dan's death was approaching. To commemorate him, I planned a special dinner. What a great opportunity to announce my surprise.

*   *   *

As I set the table on the screened porch, I chuckled to Dan. "I wish you could see how my kitchen has filled with so many vegan products—Veganaise, Smart Butter, Toffuti, agave syrup—even dairy-free ice-cream." For the meal, I prepared Indian shepherd's pie with lentils, potatoes and curry spices with a vegan lemon tart for dessert.

"Would you please open this bottle of wine," I asked Doris when she arrived promptly at six, wearing Dan's silk gingham sport coat over an old T-shirt. I was surprised when she didn't hesitate. She pulled a Swiss Army Knife from her breast pocket, and, using the corkscrew feature, expertly popped the cork.

Once we sat down, I declared I had an exciting announcement.

"I got big news too," she said, draining her wine glass and pouring herself more. I hadn't seen this bacchanalian side of her, but it seemed appropriate for the occasion, so I drained my glass too and held it out for her to refill.

"You first," she insisted.

"Okay," I said, beaming at her. "In the short time we've known each other, I've been so impressed by your work ethic and the commitment you've demonstrated to improving yourself. Since you've shown such great interest in nursing, I've decided to pay for you to take a class at the Community College to see how you like it."

"That's awful generous of you Mrs. T, but I can't accept that. First off, I don't want to be a nurse. I love being a Fig Farmer." She served herself a large plop of shepherd's pie. "My news? I been savin' for top surgery."

"Top surgery? You don't have a tumor in your breast, do you?"

"Oh no, ma'am! Nothin' like that. It's that my breasts are a burden. They keep me from feelin' like my real self. I identify as nonbinary—not male nor female inside."

"But your breasts are beautiful," I exclaimed, through pulled-back lips.

Swing Bridge

Frowning, she tugged Dan's jacket tighter around her chest. "As of today, I finally saved $10,000 to pay for a subcutaneous mastectomy and a double-incision nipple graft with liposculpture. I coulda gone cheaper, but I wanted to wait til I had enough to get 'em done right. I been goin' to Richmond on my days off for my psych evals, and today I put down my money." She took another swig of wine.

"Doris, I cannot allow you to do this." I stood up and threw down my cloth napkin. "A double mastectomy is no minor procedure, not, not—like the fig tattoo on your ankle. You have your *whole* life ahead of you—marriage, children—and this will ruin it."

Her eyes traveled slowly from where my napkin fell, to her fig tattoo, to my uncompromising gaze. "All due respect, ma'am, the decision is up to me."

We sat in angry silence until I summoned the courage to tell her about *my* decision at her age to terminate a pregnancy before we had Danny. I didn't want her to experience a life of regret.

"My top surgery's got nothin' to do with your life mistakes—I'm sicka you thinkin' you know best about how I should live."

"Is that so? I've managed to put up with you disgracing Dan's memory by wearing his suits every day, but this rudeness is more than I will tolerate. I want you out of my house."

"Done." Doris scooted her wrought-iron chair across the wooden deck, making the legs rumble like thunder.

* * *

Twenty minutes later, wrapped in the drapes again, I listened to her pickup recede down the lane. *Why are young people so stubborn, Dan?*

I kicked off my sandals, opened another bottle from Dan's wine rack, and headed down to the beach to sit on a large piece of driftwood.

Fig-Girl

The lengthening shadow from a tall row of white pines protected my pale, sagging skin from the sun as it set over Dan's grave behind the house. Laughing gulls squawked offshore like a chaotic family arguing over the dinner table. Scattered sailboats returned to their slips, disappearing single file behind Stingray Point.

When I finished the bottle, Dan asked me to dance with him in the moonlight. Gradually, he convinced me to shed my clothes to skinny dip—something I hadn't done since I was a girl. I drifted along the sandy bottom as the gentle waves lapped my shoulders, the tips of my silvery bob fanning out across the water's surface.

Dan's face smiled down from the waning gibbous moon.

Scowling back, I said, "You must be crazy if you think I'm going to apologize to that girl." I splashed him for emphasis.

Drawing a gulp of air, I rolled over to float on my back, submerging my ears to drown Dan's voice. Looking back at the farmhouse, I tried to imagine how it would feel to lose the Old Cherry Point Place. *Without a companion, I'll have to surrender someday.*

My eyelids closed. *If I apologize, Maybe Doris will come home—especially if I offer to nurse her through recovery from her top surgery.*

Tears saltier than the brackish bay water stung my crows' feet. When I opened my eyes, my own breasts startled me, floating on the surface like fresh round figs.

Diablo

MAMA PHONED EARLY Sunday morning before starting her cleaning job at the White funeral home. Most weekends I would have been dead asleep until noon, but I was watching my boyfriend snore, wondering if today I should break it off with him for good.

"Tracy, honey—" Mama couldn't wait to tell me what happened to the gay guys who lived above their hair salon in town. "—*Somebody* spray-painted dicks all over the front of Truly You Cuts & Curls last night!"

I was stoked—not because I was a hater. Me personally, I didn't care who anybody slept with. But I *did* care about a new business opportunity. A month ago, I had convinced Mama to let me use her trailer as collateral to purchase mobile blasting equipment. Now it looked like my first job was going to be a big one! I sprang out of bed to call the owners right away.

As I brushed my teeth, I remembered Mobjack High's prom was last night. I checked Instagram to confirm Mama's report. Ever since I coached the girls' softball team to the state championship last year, my feed was full of high school posts. Mama was right. I swiped through pic after pic of drunk seniors in lewd poses with the dicks—photos they would regret when they reached my age and wanted to get a business off the ground.

I tried to sound professional but I was too excited. "Hey, Bert? This is Tracy with Mobile Blasting. I heard your salon was vandalized last night?" The owners of Truly You had been doing hair in Mobjack since they moved here ten years ago when I was in the eleventh grade. Technically their names were Robert and Ernest, but everyone called them Bert and Ernie.

"Tracy?" Bert's voice sounded kind, as always, but deflated. "How are you, sweetheart?"

"I'm calling to tell you about my new dust-free blasting service, specializing in the removal of graffiti from brick and pavement. Can I stop by to give you a quote? I'm the only contractor in all of Tidewater, Virginia, with this advanced equipment."

"Oh, Tracy, you're a godsend. Yes, please, come as soon as you can. We have a terrible mess over here."

I attempted to wake my boyfriend, Trevor, to tell him I was headed out. He'd been out late doing his pirate thing for a ghost party on Wynn's Island. As a professional reenactor, he gigged all around the Chesapeake. He played Confederate and Union soldiers in Civil War naval battles, redcoats and patriots in the battle of Yorktown, a starving colonist and a Powhatan Indian at Jamestown. Once in a while he played John Smith in Pocahontas reenactments, but only if they couldn't find anyone better-looking. His favorite character was the pirate Blackbeard. He fit the part because he kept his long dirty-blond hair dyed black and his teeth were crooked.

"Get up, Trev, I have an exciting job lead." I pulled the pillow from under his head, making his Adam's apple stick up like a chicken bone, but his snoring only got louder.

Nine years ago Trevor and I went to the Mobjack prom together. We'd been a couple ever since, more on than off, I'd say. From the beginning he wanted to get married, but all these years later I still wasn't ready to commit to him because, for a grown-ass man, he didn't make enough money. *Legal* money, I should say. We relied on him to sell weed to cover our expenses whenever my construction work was unsteady. Plus, Mama hated him—except she loved his bird. It cracked her up that he had trained it to say, *"Who farted?"*

Leaving him to sleep, I pulled on my coveralls, climbed into my truck, and headed to town to cost out my first blasting job. On the way I rehearsed my pitch:

"What is mobile blasting, you ask? It's an advanced, dustless paint-removal system that's eco-friendly and will save *you* money. *How* does it save you money? By using recycled glass and water, it eliminates almost all dust and clean-up costs."

When I got to town, I let out a long whistle. Dicks everywhere. I counted six big ones in red spray paint on the brick and front door, and tons of small ones in black all over the sidewalk. No high-schoolers in sight—they must have gone home to eat their post-prom breakfasts and pass out. I parked next to Mama's Civic, the only other vehicle besides mine on the green.

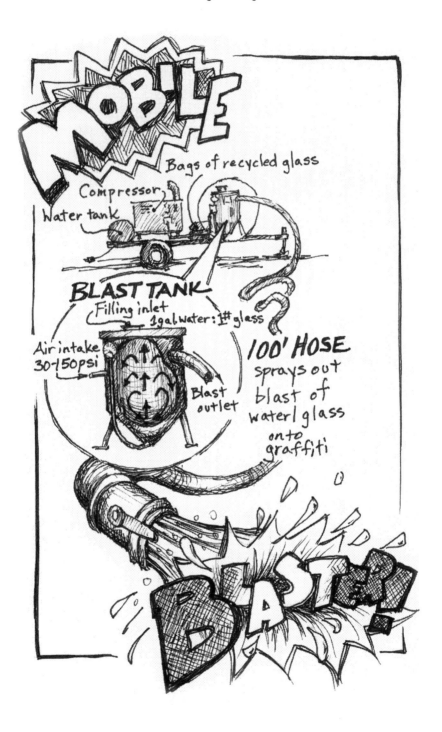

When I stepped inside Truly You, a domestic scene was in progress. Bert and Ernie looked like they wanted to kill each other. Ernie was waving a pair of hair-cutting scissors, and Bert was backed up against the shampoo bowl, prepared to defend himself with a curling iron.

"I wasn't the one who wanted to move to this shithole town," Bert yelled. "*You* wanted to come for the bird-watching."

"Shut up, Robert," Ernie growled under his pencil-thin mustache. "We have company."

"Tracy! Thank you for coming so quickly," said Bert, recovering his client charm. They both dropped their weapons and turned toward me.

"Oh my God, who's been styling your hair, honey?" Ernie asked, reaching for my ponytail to inspect the ends. Holding my jagged bangs between his fingers, he gasped, "Have you been cutting it yourself?" He sat me in his swivel chair, snapped a smock around my neck, freed my ponytail, and began spritzing.

"Who do you think trashed your place?" I asked. "Must have been a late-night prom prank, don't you think?"

"No, I *know* who did it," Bert said. "Have you seen my letters to the editor in the *Mobjack Mirror*, advocating for the removal of that Confederate statue?" I watched his reflection point to the statue on the green of a little soldier holding a rifle between his legs, hip cocked to the side, floppy hat over one eye.

I shook my head. "No, I don't read the paper." Ernie pressed his fingers into my temples to keep my head steady.

"At first lots of people disagreed with me," Bert explained. "A flurry of letters argued how we must 'preserve our history' or how 'important it is to honor military sacrifice,' yada, yada. After a while I must have convinced most folks because everyone quieted down except this one nut-bag who still refuses to admit what this is *really* about—racism. 'Anonymous' and I have been slinging letters back and forth each week for a couple of months."

Bert tossed a copy of this week's paper in my lap, folded open to the letter section.

"Do you know who Anonymous is?" I asked.

"No, but the *Mirror* knows, so I'm going to find out and get them arrested."

"You should have signed your letters 'Anonymous' too, dummy," Ernie said, his voice rising in anger again.

I read both letters aloud while Ernie layered my hair into a V-cut. Bert lit a cigarette and leaned forward from the styling chair next to mine to watch my reaction, like his letter was poetry.

"Do you have proof that Anonymous was the one who spray-painted your wall and sidewalk?" I asked. "The artwork seems pretty amateurish—no hair on the balls or veins on the—"

Bert cut me off. "No, but who else would do it? Anonymous probably paid some kids to make it look like a prom-night prank."

Ernie finished my cut, took off the smock, and began to wheeze asthmatically as he swept my hair into the corner. He excused himself to go upstairs.

"Why is he so upset?" I asked.

Bert exhaled cigarette smoke toward the Confederate statue's profile. "Oh, him. He's upset that we can't go on our cruise now. We perm old ladies' hair all year waiting for the week-long build-up to prom, which is so much fun and brings in so much business that it pays for our trip to the Bahamas every spring. This year was our best ever," he sighed.

"So why can't you go on your cruise?"

"Because now Ernest thinks we need the money to move. FBI research shows that hate crimes typically start with vandalism before escalating to violent assault. We moved here from New Jersey after our salon there was vandalized the same way. I'm tired of moving. I'm ready to stay and fight."

Ernie returned with his inhaler and they started arguing again. Me personally, I saw both sides. I wouldn't want to stay somewhere if someone hate-crimed my place—and I'd be extra salty if I had to miss my cruise because of it. But then if this happened every place I went, why keep moving?

I told them I'd be in my truck figuring their estimate. Bert nodded in my direction, but Ernie seemed like he had already left this "shithole" town and didn't care what happened to the dicks.

While I worked up my numbers, bells rang out from the Black church and the White church on opposite sides of the green, notes tumbling on top of each other like coins falling into a collection plate. Both congregations dribbled onto the green, gravitating toward Truly You to gawk at the graffiti. White church folks gathered in one clump, Black church folks stood in another, everyone shaking their heads, or clasping hands over their mouths, or muttering uh, uh, uh. None of them took selfies or seemed to find it at all funny. Exiting my truck, I made a wide arc to avoid both crowds. I didn't want to stop to talk.

Bert let me back in and locked the door. Since everyone on the green could see us through the salon windows, he invited me upstairs to talk business. Their apartment was huge—bigger than Mama's trailer *and* the house Trevor and I rented, combined. Bird paintings covered old-timey floral wallpaper as far as I could see. Ernie seemed distracted but he still took the time to show me his art studio, as if I was on a garden tour. An overstuffed armchair faced Kings Creek, where he watched herons and osprey through his spotting scope to paint them.

"My boyfriend has a bird," I said, looking at his partially finished paintings on easels around the room.

"Really? What species?" Ernie's eyebrows went up.

"Diablo is a bright-green parrot with a potty mouth."

He paused, squinting at me. "Sounds like a beautiful bird—obviously not native to *this* area." Then he excused himself, saying he had to check the cancellation policy for their cruise, throwing a nasty glance at Bert.

"How do you take your coffee, Tracy?" Bert asked.

"Do you have hot chocolate?"

Bert nodded, then disappeared into the kitchen. I felt like I was in a museum where I shouldn't touch anything or sit anywhere, so I drifted toward the living room window to watch the scene below. The sheriff had arrived to tape off the vandalized area, and the crowd was pestering him for information. Pulling up next to my truck, a reporter from the *Mobjack Mirror* hopped out of her van with a notepad and began asking bystanders for their reactions. Bert handed me a mug of hot chocolate—topped with whipped cream. He let me slurp it down before saying, "So, Tracy, what kind of money are we looking at?"

I gave him my mobile blasting pitch before handing him my estimate for $4,350. "I can start tomorrow morning if you want."

Bert's blue eyes bulged as he clutched his receding hair. "This is almost the cost of our cruise. If I manage to convince Ernest to stay in Mobjack, he's *not* going to give up his annual trip to the Bahamas. I'll have to finance this some other way."

A loud, predatory bird screech made me jump—their doorbell, apparently. "Sorry," Bert said. "We don't know how to adjust the volume." He looked down from the window. "It's the sheriff."

"About time," Ernie said, emerging from their bedroom. "I called him over an hour ago—and his office is just down the street."

I handed Bert my empty mug and told him I understood his money dilemma. "Thank you for coming over," he said, patting me on the back as we followed Ernie down the stairs. When Ernie unlocked the salon to let the sheriff in, I turned sideways and squeezed out.

Mama worked as a cleaning lady at the Black funeral home and at the White funeral home. We both thought it was strange to have separate funeral homes for Blacks and Whites, but she was glad to have two jobs instead of one. Mama always said, if anything ever happened to her, I should call the Black funeral home because they were cheaper and had better parking. When I saw her Civic was gone, I decided to stop by her place on my way home to fill her in.

Mama still lived in the trailer at the campground where I came up. The campground was on the beach with a swimming pool and other resort amenities, so my friends had always hung out at my place. Mama loved having them around—or anyone else, for that matter. She knew everyone in the county, but somehow she couldn't manage to use her social connections to get a job that paid more than minimum wage. I was all about business from the start. As a kid I collected sticks from the woods to sell to campground tourists, and I babysat my ass off. It was just me and her, so if I wanted a bike, or to go on field trips, or to buy a yearbook, I had to come up with my own money.

Mama and Trevor got off on the wrong foot when Trevor and I were in high school. Trevor always wanted two things: to be a pirate and to marry me. Mama wanted one thing: for me to do better than her in the world. Every time I saw Mama, I had to hear about her sister's kid, who had her own collections agency. Friends always asked why

Mama hated Trevor so much, but they knew why. Senior year Trevor and I were arrested for stealing copper pipes from behind the Episcopal church. Mama blamed Trevor for robbing me of some college destiny I never wanted. My dream was always to work for myself.

When I pulled up, I found Mama sitting beside the tiny pool, FaceTiming with her sister. Mama always played up the resort-like atmosphere of the campground when she talked to my aunt.

"Oh look, Tracy stopped by. I'll talk to you later." She liked to rub it in her sister's face that *her* daughter never visited.

I plopped down on the lounge chair next to Mama. "Bert and Ernie can't afford my services—$4,350."

"Honey, I know how to fix this. What we have here is a hate crime. I'll make some calls and see if we can start a 'Go Fund Me' to pay for you to remove the dicks. Like the time we raised money to send that little girl to the Miss Teen USA pageant in Texas."

*   *   *

When I got home, Trevor was making pancakes.

Stepping out of my coveralls, I hollered toward the kitchen, "You're never gonna believe what happened in town last night."

Trevor hollered back, "Did it involve red and black spray-paint?"

"So you heard. Do you know who did it?

"Why, yes, I do—hey, nice haircut," he said, stroking my hair. "But I'm gonna make *you* play twenty questions."

Trevor loved torturing me with this game, so I had gotten better at it over the years. I knew not to waste guesses on people I suspected but to narrow the field by category. After only eight questions, I was stumped: a male I knew well, living in Mobjack, under thirty, having nothing to do with prom night, with only a minor criminal record, operating alone. All the guys I knew worked in construction, but the spray-painter did not.

"Okay, I give up," I said, for the first time ever.

Trevor placed a plate of pancakes in front of me. "Diablo did it."

"What? Why would you do that to Bert and Ernie? They're so nice."

Trevor arched his eyebrow like a pirate, waiting for me to figure it out.

"You did it for me? So I could use my new mobile blaster?" I jumped up and gave him the biggest hug, screaming, "You're an awesome pirate!"

When we settled down to eat our pancakes, I said, "But I wish you hadn't picked Truly You. Ernie thinks they were vandalized because they're gay. You should have done it to the guy who owns the carwash. Now there's an asshole who deserves it."

"I didn't think that hard. It was a love crime, not a hate crime. Next time I'll get the carwash."

* * *

Mama's Go Fund Me campaign raised $4,350 in just a few hours. She started by hitting up her employers, the two biggest businesses in town. The Black funeral home put up $1,500, which the White funeral home felt obligated to match. The rest came in from smaller donations from everyone in Mobjack who loved Bert and Ernie—old ladies, parents, kids—essentially everyone with hair.

Trevor and I were watching *Pirates of the Caribbean* for the millionth time when I got a call from Bert later that afternoon.

"Mobile Blasting, Tracy speaking."

"Tracy, I have the most wonderful news. The town raised the money for you to remove the graffiti from our building."

"Awesome! I'll start first thing in the morning."

Swing Bridge

* * *

As I set up my equipment, people gathered to watch me blast the dicks. The graffiti covered a big area, so it took me most of the week to remove it. While I worked, I enjoyed watching Bert and Ernie bask in celebrity status with everyone stopping by to say how "Hate has no place in our community." The salon was booked solid for hair appointments too because everyone wanted to pump Bert and Ernie for their list of suspects. The *Mobjack Mirror* refused to reveal the identity of "Anonymous," so the crowd was left to their own sleuthing.

By the middle of the week, Bert had convinced his followers that they needed to send a strong message to whoever was responsible for this crime. "What does this heinous act call us to do?" Bert paused for effect, like a Patrick Henry reenactor. "We must remove the ultimate symbol of hate from our village green." Fired up by these words, the crowd wrangled a tarp over the little soldier's head and tied him up.

* * *

The next Sunday morning I stood back from Truly You to admire my work. Bert joined me on the green, wearing an aloha shirt. He gazed at the empty pedestal surrounded by shiny, green magnolia leaves. Pointing to where the little soldier had been, he said, "Ernest  and I stayed up late last night watching the removal of the statue." Glancing at the window above his salon, he added, "We had front-row seats from our living room." He rubbed his eyes and forehead. "I must have celebrated a little too hard—Ernest made a pitcher of his famous margaritas."

Me personally, my mission was accomplished too. All week people had been asking for my business card. Most of them needed barnacles removed from the bottoms of their boats—a new blasting service with unlimited potential!

Trevor's name never came up as a suspect. To play it safe he had avoided the green and kept quiet on social media during the whole deal. I never told anyone who did it, not even Mama, because somehow she couldn't appreciate Trevor's true pirate genius.

As I crossed the street to pack up my equipment, Bert said, "Come upstairs for some hot cocoa while Ernest cuts your check." On my way up, I used my Swiss Army Knife to remove the transformer cover and lower the volume on their doorbell. After I collected my check from Ernie and wished them a good time on their cruise, I went home to tell Trevor I was ready to marry him.

Poplar Grove

I EXHALED INTO MY truck's breathalyzer blow box, hoping mouthwash wouldn't trigger a false positive. While I waited for it to greenlight, I groped under the seat, where I kept a supply of condoms. Found some crushed fortune cookies there too. Feeling lucky, I tore one open and fished out the paper slip: *Do not mistake temptation for opportunity.* I hated getting sayings instead of fortunes, so I opened another: *A very attractive person has a message for you.* Much better.

A few minutes ago I was doodling on the want ad section of the *Mobjack Mirror* when she called.

"Nick," was all she said.

I hadn't heard anything from Lexi since the marine police arrested me for criminal trespassing at Poplar Grove. She would've been arrested too if I hadn't convinced the law I was alone. She didn't accept any of my calls during my whole legal ordeal. Not during my arraignment, not during the week of my court hearings, and not during the nine months I sat in prison thinking about her. Maybe that's why I got a DUI right after my release. Thanks to Lexi, at twenty-five I already had a decent arrest record.

Her voice still sounded throaty, a little deeper than I remembered. Sweet and relaxed, it reminded me of how she'd say my name after sex or when she wanted a backrub, a sleepy all-in-one question and command. After a long silence she whispered, "Meet me at Poplar Grove," and hung up.

Hell, I'd swim there if I had to. I slid a jimmy hat into my pocket.

Beep. My truck's V8 roared to life. I tore down the gravel lane so fast, Jojo's pack of one-eyed rescue dogs gave up the chase, barking in a thick cloud of dust.

Nobody in Mobjack had given Poplar Grove a thought in forty years, not until Lexi and I got caught living there in secret all summer. Everyone knew John Lennon and Yoko Ono had purchased the colonial plantation in 1980. They never had a chance to move in because John was murdered soon after they bought it. Yoko ended up donating the property to a local charity that couldn't afford the maintenance, so nature rewilded it.

Weaving expertly between potholes on Jojo's lane, I slapped the steering wheel to the beat of the song stuck in my head: *One thing I can tell you is you got to be free…* It was my Grandpa Chesty's music, but I loved the Beatles too. He always played it whenever we fished together.

I sometimes thought of Poplar Grove as our octopus's garden because we felt safe there after I helped Lexi escape from her psycho ex-Marine boyfriend. The only access was by water since the woods had swallowed the gravel drive. The left side of the house's wide porch and vine-covered columns sagged like a stroke victim. Spirits haunted the second floor, howling at the top of the formal staircase whenever it stormed. We used the downstairs to cook in the huge fireplace and to sleep on the screened porch, where we caught a breeze from the river every night. Down by the water's edge, inside an old tide mill, we cleared away snakes with my hunting rifle to make the loft our headquarters.

To bring in a little cash, I tried to restore the mill to working order. I wished I hadn't busted a hole in the retainer wall before I figured out the mill pond was essential. When the sluice gate opened, rushing water was supposed to turn a big wooden paddle wheel, rotating the axle that drove the gears inside the mill house to grind corn.

After the retainer wall caved, I damaged the sluice gate too. Now the only way to make the water wheel turn was to pull down on it with all my weight. We stole dent corn from a nearby farm to grind into coarse yellow flour. Lexi had the idea to call it "Antebellum Artisan Grits" and sell it to come-heres at the farmer's market on Saturdays. But after a week of me forcing the wheel, we only had a pitiful little pile of cornmeal. I was exhausted and my palms were full of splinters, so we gave up. Instead she sent me into town to sell fresh oysters from the back of my truck. The cash paid for the few things we needed—mainly soap, matches, and cooking oil. The rest of the time, Lexi worked in our vegetable garden and picked wild blueberries, while I fished for croaker, oysters, flounder, crabs, and—when we were lucky—striped bass. My Swiss Army Knife came in handy filleting the fish. Food never tasted so good.

We got away with living there until I got sloppy at the end of the summer. I set fire to my burn pile on a Monday, thinking the come-heres

had gone back to the city. Turned out *that* Monday was Labor Day. Someone called the fire department, which was all it took to ruin everything. The marine police came ashore with weapons drawn. As they cuffed me and read me my rights, I caught Lexi's eye. She was hiding in the loft of the tide mill, peeking through the tiny window. That was the last time I saw her.

Oh jeez-us fuck. My truck was on a collision course with Jojo's Camry. I stomped the brake so hard that my back end fishtailed into the ditch. Now I had to think up a good lie quick because Jojo thought my "Lexi obsession" was keeping me from getting "serious" about life. Every time I hummed a Beatles song, she knew I was thinking about Lexi, and she'd say, "Didn't you learn *anything* in prison, Nick?"

Jojo's air-conditioning didn't work, so her windows were down. Her little boy waved at me from his car seat, making me wince. I forgot I had promised to watch Damian that night while she went to a town hall meeting. She was running for a seat on the school board.

She stopped right in front of me, driver's door facing my grill like I had T-boned her. "What the hell, Nick?" She got out to inspect the angle of my back wheels. "I'm already late because I stopped to pick up Hardees for you guys."

From the ketchup all over Damian's shirt, I could see he already ate his.

Jojo and I grew up across the creek from each other, best friends at home but we hung with different crowds at school. She looked like a tall, skinny dude with a buzz cut and tats on her scalp. The left side of her face drooped like Poplar Grove from a stab wound inflicted by her daddy before he shot himself in the woods when we were thirteen.

"It's an emergency," I lied. "Chesty needs my help."

"With what?"

"Move your car forward so I can get out of this ditch. I might need you to take the wheel while I push."

She walked around to my passenger window and cupped her eyes so she could see inside. "Why are you wearing your good shirt?" she hollered through the glass.

I cracked the window. "C'mon, I need to go."

"I know you're lying, Nick. Chesty's working the sound booth for the debate tonight. I just saw him at Hardees, and he didn't say anything about needing your help."

"Okay, fine. It's none of your business where I'm going, but I'm in a hurry, so could you move?"

She opened Damian's door and took him out of his car seat. Buckling him into the passenger seat of my truck, she said, "You're going on an adventure with Uncle Nick." Then she got in her car, threw my Hardees bag out the window, and backed a quarter-mile down the lane, hitting every pothole.

I knew her meeting was important to her. A trans boy wanted to use the boys' bathroom at Mobjack High, causing everyone to lose their minds. After Jojo's injury the queer kids were the only ones who let her sit at their lunch table, so all these years later, when the bathroom issue came up, she felt a duty to defend their rights by running for the school board. She didn't expect to win, but she wanted to stir up the debate. I never figured Jojo for a politician, but she was getting all into it.

I put my truck into four-wheel drive and spun out of the ditch, facing back toward Jojo's double-wide. Since Damian had to come along, I needed to pick up some of his things to keep him busy while I was with Lexi.

"Wait here, little buddy. I'm gonna get you a clean shirt."

"I need to make a poop."

"Okay. Thank you for telling me." I tried to sound relaxed, but I was dying to get to Poplar Grove. It wasn't unusual for him to sit on the can for forty-five minutes or more.

I unbuckled him and carried him to the door so Jojo's dogs wouldn't wild him. While he sat on the potty, I gathered some of his bedtime things, thinking I'd put the passenger seat down and tuck him in for the night when I got to Poplar Grove. The September sun wouldn't set for another two to three hours, but maybe when I parked in the woods, the low light would make him think it was bedtime.

"How's it going in there," I called through the door after pacing for twenty minutes.

"Not yet."

I reached into the fridge for a beer, popped the top, and gulped it down.

Damian was singing a Beatles song, "Ob-la-di, ob-la-da…" After Jojo picked me up from prison and I moved in with them, I taught him a bunch of Beatles songs so we could sing something besides "The Wheels on the Bus…."

I reached for a second beer and drank it just as fast. After my third he announced we were out of toilet paper. He wasn't happy using a paper towel, but he could tell I didn't care. I threw a clean shirt on him and buckled him back into the truck.

Oh jeez-us fuck. The breathalyzer.

I had to wait an hour per drink before it would let me drive. I pictured Lexi, barefoot in a sundress, her wavy, caramel-streaked hair pulled to one side, waiting for me at dusk beside the mill pond.

Poplar Grove

I looked down at Damian's little rib cage. "Hey, buddy. Do you think you could do a big favor for Uncle Nick?"

He nodded eagerly.

"I need you to sit on my lap and blow into this machine as hard as you can."

After three tries—*beep*—my truck's V8 roared to life, and we were on our way down the lane again, singing "Yellow Submarine."

Turning onto the state road, I ran into traffic backed up a mile from the high school auditorium. I should have taken Jojo's jon boat to Poplar Grove, but I thought it would be quicker to park in the woods and hike in. I had no idea how many people cared about high school bathrooms. Everyone was coming into town for Jojo's debate, choking the roads with pickups, like when the A&P put all their meat on sale before going out of business.

I didn't want Lexi to get tired of waiting and leave, so I texted: *On my way.* I didn't expect a reply. She never returned my texts.

Damian tugged on my arm to play with my phone. Jojo only let him use educational apps on her phone, but I let him play *Doom* on mine. The pixelized demon scared him but he kept playing.

I hadn't returned to Poplar Grove since my arrest, but I heard the come-heres had fundraised to clean it up after my trial drew attention to its rundown condition. When I took the stand, I admitted I knew the property was a historic landmark, but I thought that was because John and Yoko had owned it. Turns out slaves built the tide mill, which produced grain that fed George Washington's troops at Yorktown during the Revolutionary War. It wasn't even the haunted old house that mattered, just the tide mill. According to the prosecutor, I caused major damage to one of five remaining tide mills in the whole country.

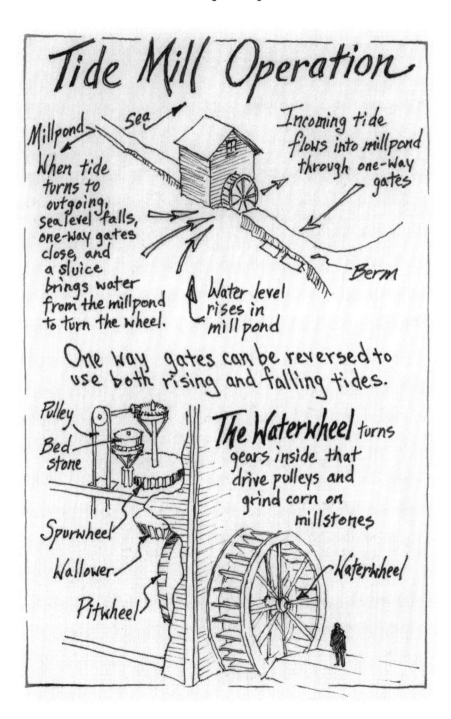

Tide Mill Operation

Sea

Millpond

Incoming tide flows into millpond through one-way gates

When tide turns to outgoing, sea level falls, one-way gates close, and a sluice brings water from the millpond to turn the wheel.

Water level rises in mill pond

Berm

One way gates can be reversed to use both rising and falling tides.

Pulley

Bed stone

Spurwheel

Wallower

Pitwheel

The Waterwheel turns gears inside that drive pulleys and grind corn on millstones

Waterwheel

I wanted to keep Lexi out of my legal mess, but my lawyer said her testimony was key to my defense. He said there was a fine line between trespassing, which is illegal, and squatting, which is not illegal in the state of Virginia. He made a big deal out of the fact that we didn't break any windows or doors to enter the house. But when the court called Lexi to testify, she failed to show up. Without her testimony my lawyer couldn't convince the judge I was playing house. Instead he bought the prosecution's argument that I was using the place as a hideout for running drugs.

The traffic started to move.

Oh jeez-us fuck. The sheriff waved me over. He wanted me to pull onto the grass inside the parking lot, so I had to open my window to explain I wasn't trying to go to the town hall meeting.

He stuck his face in my window. "Who's this young man riding without a car seat?"

I could tell he was sniffing for alcohol, so I tried not to breathe. "This is Jojo's boy, Damian. I'm babysitting."

"Where ya headed?" he asked, scanning the cab of my truck for any excuse to arrest me.

"Just drivin' around. Maybe to the lighthouse."

The line of trucks behind me started to honk while he lectured me about not having a car seat. Before letting me go, he pinned me to the headrest by pointing his fat finger in my face. "Make sure I don't find you back at Poplar Grove."

After he let me go, I made up lost time by speeding. Damian and I sang "Lucy in the Sky With Diamonds."

When I turned onto the fresh pea gravel paving the long driveway to Poplar Grove, I understood for the first time why a guy like John Lennon would have bought this place. Huge poplars lined the drive for a half-mile or so, like a proper estate. At the entrance, marked by two brick gateposts, an official plaque said Poplar Grove was on the National Register of Historic Places.

"If John Lennon hadn't been killed by that lunatic fan in New York," I explained to Damian, "he'd be an old man by now."

"Are you sure John *lemon* was the best Beatle?" He made a sour face.

"Hell yeah I'm sure. He would have played surprise concerts for us. Come-heres would have listened from their docks, and from-heres would have pulled up their fishing boats. The acoustics over the water would have been phenomenal."

Every other tree on the long driveway had a shiny new *No Trespassing* sign stapled to it. Prison hadn't changed how I felt about my right to be on this land. Come-heres thought *they* owned their slice of shoreline because they filed a deed somewhere. But my from-here ancestors had lived and died in Tidewater Virginia for sixteen generations. Hell, I grew up here before the roads had signs. I was born knowing the rhythm of the tides in every creek and inlet feeding the Chesapeake Bay. So who exactly was trespassing?

I put my truck into four-wheel drive and cut left between two poplars onto the edge of the cornfield. The farmer bushhogged an accessway twice a year to bring in his planter and harvester. I found a shady spot in the woods and pulled in.

Texted Lexi: *I'm here.*

Handing Damian my phone for something to play with, I told him to stay in the truck while I looked for somebody. He started to cry. I tucked the bottom of my pant legs into my socks. "Don't worry, it's just to avoid chigger bites," I said, kissing him on top of his head. "I'll be back in a few minutes." Outside I waved to him as I locked the doors remotely.

Poplar Grove

Approaching the house, I paused at the top of the hill to get my bearings. The place was almost unrecognizable. All our hard work making paths between the pecan orchard, rain barrels, fire pit, and rabbit traps, ruined. The old house looked sterile under several coats of white paint, and the columns seemed naked without their vines. Like suburban landscaping, half-dead grass carpets had replaced the patch of wild blueberry bushes sloping from the house to the water. The tide mill, I was glad to see, still looked the same.

I imagined Lexi watching me from the loft. To give her time to come out, I peered through the wavy glass window of the house into the room we had used as our kitchen. Newly added old-timey furniture, rugs on the wide-plank floors, and paintings on the walls made it look like a funeral home.

After a while I figured Lexi wanted me to come to her, so I headed down the lawn to the tide mill. As I reached for the wooden latch, someone inside giggled.

Lexi never giggled.

I eased backward, across the sharp oyster shells surrounding the mill house. The door flew open. Three guys sprang out, tripping over themselves as they tried to grab me. I recognized them from high school, the douchebags who harassed Jojo and the queer kids. Shoving them away, I knocked two to the ground and pushed the third into shallow water. I braced for them to come at me again but they were too drunk. They clutched their guts, laughing.

"C'mon, Nick, you know it's funny," the one in the water shouted.

Their motorboat was tied to the top bolt hinging the sluice gate. The gunwales sat below the busted retainer wall, hidden from view as the tide went out.

"We're just messing with you, dude," the one on the ground said.

Lexi and another girl stumbled out of the mill house with handfuls of beer bottles for everyone. Lexi hung back, avoiding my eyes. She looked totally different. Combat boots and a miniskirt. Hair cut short with dyed-black bangs. I squinted to make sense of her new shoulder tat: *Let it be.*

The other girl tried to give me a beer but I wouldn't take it. One of her breasts was *much* larger than the other, which distracted me.

Putting her face too close to mine, she slurred, "Lexi's with Dylan now. This was his stupid idea." More giggling.

I clenched my fists, eyes darting between Lexi and Dylan, frantic like a dumb animal that had swallowed the bait.

"Are you ticklish?" the asymmetrical girl asked, not waiting for my answer.

Suddenly everyone froze. All eyes fixed on something behind me. I hung my head and raised my arms to surrender, certain the sheriff had followed me. Strike three. Lexi and the others skittered like fiddler crabs back to their boat. I turned around, trembling, expecting to see his weapon drawn.

When I lifted my eyes, Damian stood by himself at the top of the slope.

With tremendous relief I dropped to one knee and reached toward him for a hug. He toddled down the grass like a rag doll into my arms.

As I carried him back to my truck, he clung to my neck, resting his head on my shoulder. His bottom lip quivered as we bounced along the uneven cut-through. When I pulled onto the smooth pea gravel, he started singing "Octopus's Garden."

"We don't sing that one anymore," I snapped.

Poplar Grove

While I tried to make sense of Lexi's betrayal, he fell asleep on the curvy drive back to Jojo's. Aimless and alone, I loosened my grip on the steering wheel.

The rumble strip jolted us both awake.

Approaching the high school, we ran into stopped traffic again as the town hall meeting let out. To avoid eye contact with the sheriff, I hid my face under a baseball cap, tilting the bill down. Damian's little sneakers barely hung over the seat. I reached across his lap to buckle him in, surprised he didn't weigh enough to trigger the seatbelt alarm.

That's when I noticed. He had carefully tucked his pant legs into his socks. I imagined his little fingers trying to protect his ankles, taking his time to do it right, then unlocking the heavy door, using his feet to push it open, sliding on his belly all the way to the ground, alone in the dark woods, searching for me.

I tossed the cap behind my seat and started teaching Damian "Fool on the Hill." Both of us smiled at the sheriff. He waved us through.

Dragon Run

THE RUSTY TEXACO STAR clung to its pedestal above Main Street, welcoming me back to my hometown. Beneath, a brightly painted visitor center had displaced the long-defunct filling station where we used to smoke cigarettes. I strained to see the bones of Mobjack Courthouse under a veil of self-conscious updates, like sidewalk bump-outs planted with native seagrasses. *Were they expecting tourists?*

The drive from Brooklyn to the western shore of the Chesapeake Bay was just long enough to finish my audiobook on empty-nest syndrome. "Wake up, Brooke." I tapped my sleeping daughter's knee in the passenger seat of our rented SUV. She was wearing her orange Princeton hoodie, like she had every day since her acceptance last spring.

Swing Bridge

"Mom, *please* call me Khady," Brooke said, rubbing her eyes under her glasses. That was the Senegalese name my adopted African American daughter had chosen for herself to start college. I had no objection to her name change, but the transition was hard for me.

"Look." I pointed. "Lucky's Diner is still here!" I pulled to the curb. "Let's grab a bite."

After a spine-popping stretch, I tugged my tank top down to reach my leggings. Brooke trained her handheld movie camera on me, asking how it felt to be back in Mobjack. "Like my arms are too pale for late summer," I said, pulling my gray bob into a ponytail.

Everyone looked up when we entered the restaurant. The place was plastered in '50s nostalgia, just the way I remembered it from the '70s. The smells of fried fish and crab cakes triggered memories of humid, buggy summers on the water. An elderly from-here playing solitaire behind the counter pointed to a booth that was freeing up. I erased the wrinkles from around her watery blue eyes to see if she was somebody I knew. Nothing registered.

A waitress with a mullet approached our booth. As a teenager in the '80s, I had experimented with a mullet—the perfect hairstyle to express my bisexuality. I'd still have one today if the New York fashion police would allow it. Reaching across the Formica tabletop, I pushed Brooke's camera into her lap, stage-whispering over a Johnny Cash song, "It's rude to film in the restaurant."

"Y'all decided on whatcha gonna have?"

In a local accent I thought I had lost, I said, "Yes, ma'am, I'd like the fried *oyshters* with a side of collards." Brooke's mouth flew open with a horsey snort. Scowling, I handed both menus back, saying in an exaggerated New York accent, "And she'll have da chicken Caesar—no croutons."

Brooke's perfect white teeth gleamed when she laughed, reassuring me her braces were worth the financial stretch. Her face turned serious. "Mom, I want to ask you something."

I knew I didn't want to hear this by the way she sat on her hands and hunched her shoulders. "Do *not* tell me you forgot some piece of film equipment. The last electronics store was—"

"No, no—that's not it. I want you to consider something."

I folded my arms. "Consider what?"

"Since we're here, what if I made a documentary about you reconciling with your father?"

"Oh my god, Brooke." I lunged forward, jostling the condiment caddy. "We came all this way so you can make a documentary about Dragon Run. Do *not* tell me you've changed your mind." My back thumped against the cherry-red seat as I refolded my arms.

"*Khady,*" she said in a hushed tone, glancing around to see if people were staring. "If you're going to drag me into these all-White spaces, can you at least not make a scene?"

I should have known. Ever since she found a spider's nest in her sleeping bag on that Unitarian camping trip, her curiosity about nature had turned to disgust. She had sweet-talked me into this trip, saying she wanted to make a documentary about a place she knew was special to me. A series of coincidences had protected the Dragon Run water-shed from human impact for over four hundred years, keeping it much the way John Smith encountered it in 1607. My

father and I used to canoe to the headwaters to pick mushrooms and marvel at the ancient swamp cypresses.

"I knew your first reaction would be *no*," she continued, recording our conversation like always. The summer before her junior year, I helped Brooke apply for funding to make a film about Goree Island in Senegal, the largest slave trading center on the African coast. Her film won a major competition and was screened at the New York Film Center where she met her idol, Spike Lee. He urged her to take her film equipment everywhere and record everything. At first, the intrusion of her camera in our everyday lives had annoyed me, but I learned to live with it.

"All I'm asking is for you to *consider* reconnecting," Brooke pleaded. "Twenty-five years is a long time. Wouldn't you want *me* to forgive *you*?"

The idea of my father had always intrigued Brooke. As a child, she would fall asleep asking questions like *What was his favorite book? How did I think he would die?* I expected her to ask about *her* birth family, but she never did.

"If I say I'll consider it, I'm afraid I'll raise false hopes. That chapter of my life is closed."

"Please?" She put her camera down and pressed her hands together, the way she used to beg for more screen time when she was little.

"Fine," I said, shaking my head no, like a hostage.

The mullet appeared with our plates. Brooke always ordered the same Caesar salad in every restaurant, while I tried local specialties. She declared her salad substandard. My oysters tasted sweet, like summers from childhood before I knew my father's love was so fragile.

* * *

Tall cedars lined a long gravel lane, creating a grand approach to a historic property known as Seven Oaks. I would have recognized any of Mobjack's majestic homes from the water, but I had never been inside one. Up close, paint peeled from columns, plantation shutters dangled, and a few balusters were missing from the second-floor balcony.

"Look at this place," Brooke said. "I bet they had slaves."

"Might have. The description said the house was built in 1813 by a doctor who traveled by boat to reach his patients."

I found the key box and punched in the Airbnb code while Brooke sat on the porch swing, twisting her budding locks with her right hand and filming my activity with her left. Brooke and I didn't need a place that could sleep twelve, but the listing showed kayaks available, and hurricane season rates made it affordable.

While I dragged stuff in from the car, Brooke explored, hollering from upstairs, "I call the Doctor's Suite."

"Like hell you do," I hollered back, anticipating the moment when she would discover the house had no Internet.

A librarian at Brooklyn College, I had plenty of opportunity to gather research for Brooke's project. I spread my colorful maps and scientific studies across one end of the long dining room table. The Field Guide to Virginia Fungi reminded me of how scared I was whenever my father would eat mushrooms from the banks of Dragon Run. I had always nodded when he explained how to tell the edible ones like oyster mushrooms and true morels from death caps, but they looked way too much alike for my comfort.

As I stocked the fridge with organic vegetables from our food co-op at home, the sky darkened, and breakers advanced toward the pier like warriors.

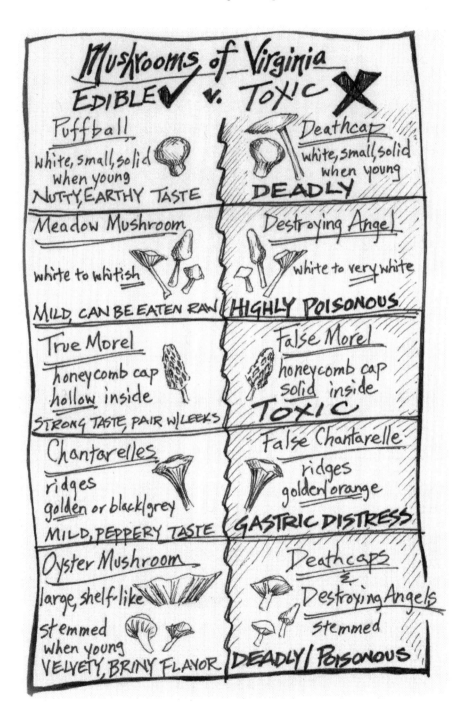

"Brooke! Come help me finish unloading the car. It's about to pour."

"Khady! What? Nooooo!"

There it was.

"It's just one week," I apologized. "You'll survive."

That night, hail pelted the metal roof as gale-force winds took down power lines, leaving us without electricity. Waves crashed over the riprap, submerging the pier and flooding the lawn. Brooke and I ended up sharing the king-sized bed in the Doctor's Suite because neither of us wanted to be alone during the storm.

I rose early and decided to brave my way into town to pick up breakfast. Mobjack Courthouse was deserted in the blackout. I kept driving, remembering how my father would clutch his shortwave during storms. I saw lights at the general store where I used to buy candy, so I stopped in for homemade muffins, the local newspaper, and—oh thank god—hot coffee.

Back at the house, Brooke had set up her mobile editing studio at the other end of the dining room table. I stood behind her chair, reliving our harrowing drive down the New Jersey Turnpike.

"Maybe the weather will clear this afternoon, and we can try out the kayaks," I suggested on my way to the kitchen to find plates for our muffins. The rattling windows didn't justify optimism. "Or we could tour the historic triangle—Yorktown, Jamestown, and Williamsburg."

"Those places where people dress up like slaves and masters?"

"No," I corrected. "Those are the James River plantations. These people dress up like Native Americans and colonists."

"Isn't there a Starbucks around here with Wi-Fi and electricity? I'm going to need to charge my equipment soon."

"Let's go to the library after breakfast because the…"

Brooke finished, "…measure of a community is its public library."

I slid a lemon poppyseed muffin toward her, handing over a section of the *Mobjack Mirror*. Looking at the obituaries, I commented, "This woman passed away after a long career as a professional bra-fitter at Mobjack's department store—I remember that witch!"

Brooke swallowed the last of my coffee. "Mom?" She was sitting on her hands again.

"Oh no, what now?"

"I didn't want to tell you yesterday because I wasn't sure how you would take it."

"Take *what*?"

"You know how your father sends letters every so often?"

"Every April, for my birthday, but I never respond."

"That's what I wanted to talk to you about—last spring, I responded."

"To my father?" I choked on my bran muffin. "You had no right to—"

"I knew you'd be mad, but I felt so sorry for him, always writing about the weather and hoping you'll visit. I wanted him to know about *me*."

"Oh, Brooke…" I reached into my backpack for my water bottle.

"Khady," she whispered. "He was so excited about my film idea that he sent money for all of this film equipment."

"I thought you bought this stuff with money you made from tutoring."

"You have no idea how much this stuff costs." She thrust her neck toward me. "I have over three thousand dollars of professional equipment here. But you'll like this—he wants to help pay for Princeton!"

"You've been taking money from my father behind my back? How often do you two communicate?"

"I dunno, once a week? Grampa's too old to text, so we talk on the phone."

"*Grampa?* Oh my god, Brooke, this is too much." I jammed my arms into my wet raincoat.

"Still Khady," Brooke mumbled. "Don't forget you promised to *consider* reconnecting."

I slammed the heavy wooden door behind me.

* * *

Later that evening, I boiled pasta on the gas stove and left a bowl for Brooke. She spent the day in front of a mirror in the entry hall, practicing her hip-hop moves in dim natural light with no music. I crashed early to read by flashlight until my batteries weakened and died.

Wide awake in the darkness, I listened to the storm beat against the wavy glass, imagining conversations between my father and daughter. He raised me to be like him, a self-reliant survivalist. I raised Brooke to be open-minded so she could rely on the strength of a community. My father taught me to catch eels for bait and read the water as we picked our way through the Dragon's muddy channels, as if my livelihood would depend on it. I taught Brooke to read people, and how to navigate socially for the same reason.

I fell asleep just before dawn, dreaming about how angry my father was when he discovered my lesbian poetry. When I awoke, it was late morning. The clock radio was blasting static, red numerals flashing like the bodega lights outside my window at home. Relieved to have power back, I went downstairs to brew my Zabar's Ethiopian blend.

Cradling my coffee, I found Brooke asleep on a couch in the den. "Good morning sleepyhead," I said, patting her shoulder. She squinted, groping for her glasses. "It's still pouring, but the power's back on."

"Yeah, Grampa says it's a nor'easter." She yawned.

I flinched at her casual mention of him. "Get dressed," I snapped. "We're going to the lighthouse."

The ditches overflowed, blurring the edges of the road. I strained to see the yellow center line through the frantic wipers. "Why," I began, "is it so important to have a relationship with the Captain?"

"You mean Grampa?" Her camera was recording.

"He used to make everyone—including his daughter—call him Captain. Can you explain what led you to contact him?"

"I always wanted to be part of a big family, spending summers the way you did—with chaotic meals at a long farm table."

"Why would you think he's the key to that dream? He's the most solitary person you could ever meet. The stories I've told you about large family gatherings were from when he was at sea, and I stayed with the neighbors, sometimes for months."

"He obviously cares about you," Brooke said, eyeing me through her viewfinder. "Why else would he keep sending letters and offering to pay for stuff?"

"Stubborn, I guess. Trust me, his love—and money—required me to pretend I'm someone I'm not. Frankly, I can't believe he's so accepting of a Black granddaughter."

Arriving at the promontory facing the lighthouse, I cut the ignition.

"Well, he doesn't exactly *know* I'm Black."

I stiffened.

"I wanted him to know 'the content of my character' before he judged 'the color of my skin.'"

The cattails lay flat in the wind driving across the marsh. I remembered how I had waited as long as possible to tell the Captain about my girlfriend.

Dragon Run

The shape of the lighthouse was hard to make out through the storm. Everyone who grew up in Mobjack knew the story of how the hurricane of 1933 left it isolated from the mainland, perched in solitude on rocky stubble. I reached across the console to fish my Swiss Army Knife from my backpack.

"Would you ever consider forgiving him?" she asked, aiming her camera in my face.

"There's nothing to forgive." Unfolding the largest blade to cut slices of cheese and apple for our breakfast, I handed her a slice of Gouda on my index finger. "I've accepted who he is and moved on, and you should too."

We ate in silence, watching the bay churn. The windshield framed the dramatic scene, like a black-and-white clip from a Bergman film. Brooke turned off her camera and traced a single raindrop down the window with her fingernail.

Turning the car around, I said, "Let's be grateful for what we *do* have—each other and an exciting film project planned as soon as this weather clears. How 'bout going to the movies this afternoon?"

Brooke leaned forward and sat on her hands for the third time in as many days.

"What the hell now?" I slammed the brakes and pulled over.

"Grampa invited us to come to his house this afternoon, and I told him we would."

"Let me get this straight," I exploded. "You duped me into coming down here by saying you wanted to make a film about the Dragon so you could film me reconnecting with him?"

"No, Mom. I really *do* want to make the Dragon Run film. But I also want to make this one." More pleading hands. "Please say we can go."

Swing Bridge

"Absolutely not." I pulled back onto the slick road to return to our Airbnb. "Tell him we're *not* coming."

* * *

When Brooke came down the stairs wearing the white dress and low heels we had purchased for her acceptance speech when she won the film competition, I realized she intended to keep her appointment with the Captain. Her defiant look dared me to stop her.

"This has gone too far, Brooke. I need you to be smarter than this, or I won't be able to trust you away at college."

"For the last time, it's Khady. I need *you* to stop suffocating me, Mom!" She snatched the rental car key.

Desperate to protect her, I grabbed the hood of her raincoat, yanking her head back. She swung around in a rage, raising her fist at me.

Our eyes locked, until I let go.

* * *

The empty house felt cold and lonely. I decided to build a fire in the wood stove. I found dry logs in the woodshed, and plenty of small sticks downed by the storm. Smoke filled the house as I fanned the kindling with A Naturalist's Guide to Butterflies. My mind traveled to the Captain's den, where a brass mariner's clock chimed every fifteen minutes, keeping his home on land as shipshape as his life at sea.

I had worked so hard to protect Brooke from people like the Captain. To my knowledge, she hadn't experienced overt racism yet because I raised her in a multicultural open-hearted lesbian community.

The front door flew open.

Brooke sloughed her raincoat to the floor. "What happened?" I asked, jumping to my feet. "Are you okay?" I followed her to the living room couch.

She pulled her knees to her forehead and sobbed, "You were right. I never should have gone there. I should have listened to you."

"Tell me what happened," I said, rubbing her back. "You weren't gone very long."

"I don't want to talk about it, or think about it, ever again. Here." She handed me her camera. "Watch for yourself. I filmed the whole thing!" Gripping the banister, she disappeared upstairs.

I fumbled with the camera's menu to figure out how to play back footage on the tiny screen. *Here we go.* I recognized the lane leading to my old house in Horn Harbor. The Captain emerged from the kitchen, bent with age, stomping across the gravel toward the camera, yelling something I couldn't make out. When he got closer, the microphone picked up "stolen belongings" and "going to file a sheriff's report." Brooke's silence enraged him. He accused her of being "too stupid to speak." The camera shook as he said, "This is why we can't trust you people." His face fell. "Wait, who are you?" he demanded.

My daughter's voice was faint, but clear. "I'm your granddaughter."

The camera swirled as she got back into the rental. My father slapped the passenger window, insisting she come into the house, repeating, "Brooke, I didn't realize..."

The screen went black.

I dropped the camera and hiked the stairs, two at a time, to comfort my daughter. At the landing, I stepped over her discarded outfit and knocked gently on the bathroom door. Sloshing bathwater stilled to an echoing drip.

"Khady?" I called from the other side. No response. I slumped down the wall, missing the days when I could make everything okay for her.

Finally, I gathered her clothes, folded them, and left them in a neat stack on the newel post. "I'm downstairs if you need me."

Swing Bridge

In my absence, my fire had gone out. With only one match left, I looked around for more paper. Crumpling my maps, directions, and studies, I placed them under the wet twigs and struck the last match.

The paper caught, and the stove's cavity roared to life. After a brief display, the blaze shrank, and charred flakes spiraled up the flue. Without more matches, I felt helpless to do anything but watch. As I was about to turn away, an underlying twig ignited and slowly passed its flame to higher ones.

Khady came downstairs in her pajamas and sat on the bench beside me. To my surprise, she left her camera on the couch where I had dropped it. I wrapped my arm around her. We sat together in silence, watching the bright orange glow blacken the stove's glass door, then burn away the creosote.

*　*　*

Early the next morning, the storm released its grip on Mobjack, moving down the Bay. I lifted the window sash, filling the Doctor's Suite with the fresh scent of salt air and pine forest. Though the tide was out, the sparkling creek swelled with rainwater. It would have been a perfect day to paddle to the headwaters of Dragon Run.

Rescue Squad

BOZWELL HAD BEEN DRINKING all day, and my EMT license was suspended, so we had no business answering the call in the first place. We reached the scene in eight minutes. He said he had to pee. Sure. Fine. When I found the pregnant lady, she was already in the dorsal lithotomy position with the head beginning to crown. I texted Boz, *TOO LATE FOR TRANSPORT!* My first delivery. I laid out the towel, scissors, and umbilical clamp for Boz and began timing the contractions. *3 MINUTES APART.* The lady screamed, "Girl, get me some goddamn help!" *Where* was Boz? When the purply head came out, my panic surged and I radioed for backup. A minute later the whole baby slid into my arms. I was afraid something awful had happened to Boz, but when backup arrived he acted like he had been in charge all along. I covered for him, of course, but I wanted to kill him.

That night my boyfriend, Zach, insisted I tell the Squad's board of directors about Bozwell drinking on the job. We were pet-sitting a border collie in a swanky waterfront home where every room smelled like pet stain remover. I tossed around all night, trying to find the guts to confront Boz privately so he wouldn't be fired. I wanted to wait until after the Squad's fundraising gala because I couldn't imagine a successful event without him. But after yesterday I had no choice. Someone might have died.

I should have demanded an explanation from Boz on the drive back to the Squad but I was too shaken. Besides, who was I to criticize Dr. Kenneth Bozwell? He was so much more than my boss at the Mobjack Rescue Squad. He was a decorated EMS hero, a deacon at church, and a retired philosophy professor. On top of all that, he was Santa Claus. The Mobjack Christmas Committee chose him every year to lead the Christmas parade down Main Street in his custom-made velveteen suit, even though he was tall and thin with slicked-back silver hair, blue eyes, and a dimpled chin. A breath mint stayed tucked in his cheek, giving him the smell of candy canes all year round.

Zach and I had lived like nomads for two years since high school, but I still hated waking up in someone else's house every morning. To make each place feel homier, Zach displayed our framed prom photos and stuffed sea-mammal collection on the bedside tables. We started our pet-sitting business to save for our own place where we could adopt all the rescue pets we wanted. He worked as a groomer at Happy Paws, handing everyone our card. The from-heres didn't need pet-sitters because family would help, but the come-heres hated to send their pets to a kennel, so Zach and I had no trouble bouncing from one fancy beach house to the next.

At first we felt sorry for our clients, having to throw money at every problem, but it didn't take long for us to become spoiled too. Zach came out of the bathroom wearing a silk robe, smelling like eucalyptus body lotion. I headed downstairs to see what delicacy I could forage for breakfast.

I hoped wearing my EMT uniform would remind everyone at the Squad that office work was not what I trained for. During my probation I reported to Dr. Bozwell in the business office to help with whatever he needed. I excelled as the only female from my class at Mobjack High to pass the EMT course and get hired to work at the Mobjack Rescue Squad. From my cohort almost everyone quit in the first year due to high stress and low pay, but I loved the excitement of answering the call. I had wanted to be a first responder ever since my father died in the line of duty as a member of the Coast Guard.

Zach joined me in the kitchen, dressed for work in his pawprint scrubs. "You're gonna do it today, right? I—"

"Yes," I cut him off, tired from no sleep. "Where's the stuff we printed last night?"

While he went back upstairs to get the list of Virginia rehabs, I continued my search for breakfast. I found one Dove Bar left in the freezer and wondered if Zach had eaten the rest. He was always trying to lose weight, and I was always trying to gain some.

"Why do *you* have to take him?" Zach asked, returning to the kitchen. "Doesn't he have anyone else?"

"Who knows?" I said, checking the weather on my phone. "He's from the don't-ask-don't-tell era." The August humidity fogged the floor-to-ceiling windows, making the house feel like a terrarium. "He lives on his sailboat with his cat, Brunnhilde."

"That's so sad," Zach said, eating maraschino cherries from the jar. I knew Zach felt sorry for me too, having no family left in Virginia since my dad died. Zach and I both loved his big, loud family, which is why we never wanted to leave Mobjack.

Zach and the border collie stood in the doorway to see me off. I stomped on the kick start of the Suzuki Motocross bike I bought from my EMT partner, Brandon. The bike was his graduation present, but after he got drunk and broke the taillight, his father made him sell it cheap. His loss was my gain, which really pissed him off. To get me back, he told Bozwell about me using a defibrillator on a fox after a hawk attack. That was *after* my two prior warnings not to use Squad equipment to rescue animals. The board wanted to fire me, but Boz protected me out of respect for my dad.

Dr. Bozwell had slipped his little red convertible into the Squad's only shady parking spot. He liked to arrive early to play ping-pong with the EMT guys before retreating into his office. My first stop was always the restroom—if I didn't wet down my short, blond helmet hair, it would stick up all day, and the guys would call me "toilet brush." The Squad didn't have a women's room, so I banged on the door to make sure it was unoccupied. Splashing my hair and face with cold water, I closed my eyes and hoped Boz wouldn't make this harder than it had to be.

When I cracked open the door to Boz's office, I noticed he wasn't playing his opera music. He loved it so much that sometimes he would stop in the middle of a conversation, close his eyes, and hum with the soprano in his low, gravelly voice.

"Dr. Bozwell?" My voice sounded warped, like I was underwater.

Rescue Squad

"Morning, Jessie," he said, scowling at his computer. He was usually clean-shaven, with a crisp, white polo bearing the Squad's logo tucked into a pair of cargo shorts. But this morning he looked rough, still wearing his navy-blue EMS T-shirt from yesterday's run, reminding me mine was wadded up in my locker, covered in afterbirth.

Staring at the coffee mug on his desk, I asked, "Can I talk to you privately?" My heart was racing.

"Can it wait?" It was more an order than a question.

"I guess," I mumbled, disappointed not to have it over with.

Dr. Bozwell's office was knee-deep in stuff. *Interesting* stuff that he magnet-fished from the floor of the Chesapeake Bay, like old coins, oyster knives, a boat throttle from a shipwreck, a swivel pulley, and skeleton keys, mixed with *boring* stuff, like EMT shift schedules, training manuals, run sheets, and expense reports. Two trails bisected the heap, one from his desk to the door and the other from his desk to my desk. If someone knocked, he would wedge himself in the doorway to block the view and talk—sometimes for an hour.

I felt special, getting to spend so much time with Dr. B in his inner sanctuary. His walls were plastered with appreciation awards for his heroic water rescues. My favorite was the one with an inlaid photo of him dangling from a helicopter.

I had discovered his drinking problem two weeks ago. Bozwell stepped out of the office, leaving me to print labels for the gala invitations. When the label-maker jammed, I used my Swiss Army Knife to gouge out the crumpled labels. In search of a new roll, I went behind his desk. Instead of office supplies, I found the cabinets crammed with empty liquor bottles. I thought he was a caffeine addict, drinking coffee all day. I picked up his coffee mug and tasted its cold contents. After I choked and gagged, a fiery scorch sank down my esophagus.

When I told Zach that night, we had our first big fight. He thought it was a huge mistake to protect Boz by keeping his secret. "Covering for a guy like him will backfire in your face." I accused Zach of not understanding Squad loyalty.

My phone pinged in my back pocket with a text from Zach. *How did it go?*

I texted back, *Haven't done it yet. He's busy with something.*

Dr. Bozwell waved me to his desk. "Jessie, I need a big favor. Can you help me erase this hard drive? I'm giving this computer to someone soon, and I don't want them to have access to my files."

"Are you sure?" I asked, knowing I would make a backup on a flash drive in case he changed his mind. "A quick erase takes about two hours, but if you want to do it right, it'll take about three days."

"Do the quick one, please."

While I downloaded a free data destruction program, he left and returned with a box of Hefty trash bags. He scooped the boring stuff into bags and piled the interesting stuff against the walls.

"What's going on, Dr. B?" I was beginning to worry that something besides his drinking was wrong. He opened the supply cabinet and raked out the empties, unconcerned about the deafening clinking noises. Then he reached into his leather satchel, opened the seal on a new bottle, and poured a shot into his coffee mug without bothering to add coffee.

While I waited for his data to wipe, I helped him carry seven overstuffed bags to the Squad's truck. I felt like I was tracking a wild animal. "Dr. B, there's something we have *got* to talk about."

"Can it wait? I need you to take this stuff to the dump." He threw me the keys. "I've got a couple of errands to run, and then I promise you'll have my full attention."

Rescue Squad

As part of my suspension, I was not allowed to drive any of the Squad's vehicles, but if Boz told us to do something, we did it. Even Brandon would break a rule if Boz told him to. Boz's authority outranked EMS protocols, board decisions, and ER doctor orders.

Mobjack had the most beautiful dump, cool and shady. Zach and I joked that it was perfect for camping. Bayberries, tulip poplars, and red maples surrounded the recycling bins. When I pulled up, the attendant, Wanda, came out to help. I flushed with frustration when I realized Boz hadn't sorted the trash for recycling. Wanda opened each bag to separate the paper, cardboard, plastic, and glass.

"Must have been some party at the Squad," Wanda said, holding Wild Turkey bottles in each hand.

I nodded, not wanting to encourage questions.

"Lookie here—throwing away unopened bills and bank statements?"

She had me pull the truck over so others could get by while she combed through the trash, taking her time to study the contents.

When I finally returned to the Squad, Bozwell's car wasn't there. I forgot to take my swipe card with me, so I had to ring the buzzer. Boz had installed an electric door lock after the board learned about the community bringing their injured animals to the Squad.

Brandon's voice came over the speaker. "What do you want?"

"C'mon, Brandon. Let me in."

He was pissed because I had hung a dead opossum with a cranial fracture in his locker as payback. Before he opened his big mouth, the board hadn't thought to create a policy *forbidding* the treatment of animals, and Boz had looked the other way. Now, when people left critically injured animals on the Squad's doorstep, I had to watch them die.

Brandon left me outside like one of those poor animals. I buzzed and buzzed until I gave up and sat on the stoop in the blazing sun, waiting for Boz to return. After an hour or so, his little red convertible drifted into the parking lot, top down, rolling to a slow halt. Showered and shaved, Boz looked late for Pride Week, wearing a striped sailor shirt, sunglasses, and a scarf around his neck. *He must be really drunk now,* I thought.

"Hop in, Jessie. Let's go to the beach where you can talk to me privately."

I knew better than to get in the car with someone who had been drinking, but since it was Boz, my obedience was automatic. Boz was the one who accompanied me to Washington, DC, where President Obama awarded me Dad's Medal of Honor after Dad drowned rescuing a Navy pilot who crashed in the Bay near the Mobjack lighthouse.

The paved road ended at the sand. After we got out of the car, I couldn't wait one more minute. "Dr. Bozwell, I believe you have a drinking problem, and we need to get you help."

He gazed at the horizon for a while, weaving like an inflatable yard decoration. After a long minute he patted my shoulder. "You've got real guts to say that."

"Don't worry, I won't tell anyone. I have a list of rehab facilities."

Giving him a moment, I stepped into the marsh grass to pick up a stranded horseshoe crab, setting her down with her legs on the wet sand. We watched as she found her way back into the water.

"You're just like your father, Jessie, a born rescuer." Taking off his penny loafers, he said, "Let's walk in the surf. This may be my last chance to mentor you for a long time."

It felt odd to take off my steel-toed boots in the middle of the day to walk on the beach. I expected him to be embarrassed, but instead he acted like this was some sort of training exercise for me.

As I trailed behind he asked, "Do you know what Euripides said about loyalty?"

"No, sir." *Not another philosophy lecture.*

"He said, one—" Boz stopped short and I almost bumped into him. Crouching in the sand, he picked up a piece of iron ore and brushed it off. "This'll give you some perspective—a souvenir from when a meteor created the Chesapeake Bay thirty-five million years ago." He handed me the rusty-orange fragment with his scarred and calloused hand.

I held the heavy lump, distracted for a moment by its porous crannies.

"Drinking is the least of my problems." He paused to wipe the lenses of his sunglasses with his scarf. "If I stick around I'm going to be arrested for embezzlement."

"That's crazy," I blurted. "You would never do anything like that." I checked his eyes to see if he was kidding but he looked lost. Boz was the one who saved our Squad when, all across the country, small-town volunteer rescue squads were folding due to a diminishing number of volunteers. He had applied for nonprofit status, filled the board with his come-here cronies, and organized our first annual gala to raise funds to pay the EMTs.

"You bet I did. You're an embezzler too but a much smaller one." His hand pressed my back to make me continue walking. "When you started using the Squad's equipment to rescue animals, the board noticed that medical supplies were over budget. I thought installing the electric lock would solve it, but the board decided we were past due for an audit."

"Am I in trouble too?" My jaw was trembling.

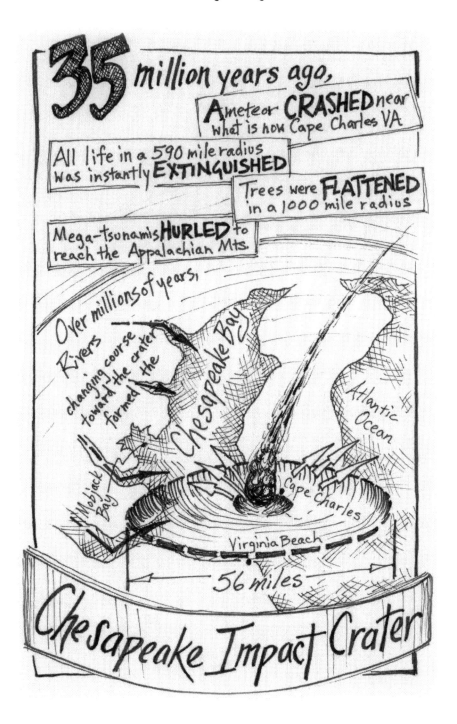

"Of course not. I would never let anything bad happen to you." He licked his dry lips.

"What did you need the Squad's money for?" I asked, hoping for an explanation that would preserve my faith in him.

"My own hubris, I suppose."

As he blabbed on about the ancient Greeks, my pulse raced. He had asked *me* to erase his hard drive and throw away the bags of evidence, which I did out of dumb loyalty. Watching his mouth move, I felt terror and despair for both of us.

Then, like the sudden resuscitation from a chest compression, my training kicked in. The golden rule for EMTs: Personal safety comes first because we're no help to anyone if we *become* a victim. My hero was drowning but I had made a backup of his files that would save me.

We reached the end of the sandbar. The tide was going out, leaving small shimmering pools on the land. I turned back, walking a little ahead to coax Boz along. He dawdled like a child, playing in the sand, throwing shells in the surf.

When we finally returned to the jetty to put our shoes and socks back on, Boz turned serious. "Jessie?" He waited for me to make eye contact before saying, "If you drive me to my boat, I'll let you keep the BMW as my thanks."

I nodded. He dropped his keys into my sweaty palm.

As I drove, Bozwell blasted his opera music with eyes closed. He didn't notice when I drove past his marina, turning toward the Squad.

I slammed on the brakes. A huge crowd had gathered in the parking lot. Boz's eyes flew open as his hands braced against the dash. A local news truck with an extended antenna loomed over the scene. Five cruisers with lights flanked the entrance. The sheriff used his PA system to order me to proceed while the crowd chanted,

"Shame, Shame, Shame." I was surprised to see some of the same people who had dropped by yesterday to flirt with Boz and ask him for favors—like the chair of the Oyster Festival, who wanted him to supply an ambulance for her event, or the member of the Lions Club who asked him to judge their Chili Cook-off.

"I'm sorry," I said to Boz, trying to hand him his keys. "You were my hero."

The sheriff removed him from the car, handcuffed him, and read him his rights. Two deputies escorted me to an adjacent patrol car, saying they needed to question me at the station. Bozwell forced a smile for the crowd, a sad reminder of how he had led so many Christmas parades down Main Street.

"Don't worry," I called from the backseat of my patrol car. "I'll take care of your cat."

*　*　*

I finally made it back to Zach after dark that night. "Were you worried?" I asked. I hadn't checked in with him since that morning.

"I knew something crazy was going down," he said, removing the bungee cords holding the cat carrier on the back of my bike. Brunnhilde, who had been yowling in distress the whole ride, began purring when Zach held her to his chest. "Everyone heard Wanda's call to the Sheriff on the police scanner. Then Mobjack Talk blew up with photos of Bozwell in handcuffs. The auditors are saying he embezzled over two hundred thousand dollars."

While Zach grilled Omaha steaks on the outdoor grill, I recounted every detail of the day.

After dinner we floated in the hot tub built into the deck, like a jimmy and a sook bubbling in a pot. He handed me a cigar and held out a torch lighter while I rotated the end for a uniform, amber glow. Then he lit one for himself and asked, "Did he ever tell you what Euripides had to say about loyalty?"

"Oh, yeah—something about, 'one loyal friend is worth ten thousand relatives,'" I puffed.

Zach's laughter turned to choking.

I stretched for my pants hanging on the railing to search the pockets for the chunk of iron Boz gave me on the beach. Handing it to Zach, I said "This'll give you some perspective—a souvenir from when a meteor created the Chesapeake Bay thirty-five million years ago."

As he inspected the meteorite's crannies, I slipped out an apology for my role in our fight. Sinking lower to let the jets massage my shoulders, I said, "It's funny. This morning? I would have done anything for Boz."

Sail Forth

WIDE AWAKE, watching the strawberry moon rise and set over the tidal creek outside my bedroom window, I replayed the scene from yesterday in my mind. I couldn't blame my insomnia on my ex-husband's snoring anymore. Nor could I blame it on waiting for my daughter to return from a faraway sailing regatta. Both had moved out last fall, leaving me alone in the oversized house.

A harrowing screech tore open the night. Gunshots and a string of profanity followed the gruesome sounds of a fox attack on my neighbor's chickens. They must have forgotten to lock the coop again. I rose to slam my window closed.

Giving up on sleep, I wrapped myself in my terry cloth robe and slippered downstairs to make a mug of instant. I couldn't be bothered to brew the perfect cup at home. Not since I started managing my soon-to-be former father-in-law's gourmet coffee shop in town, across from his law office.

I caught my breath.

Just my own reflection in the glass doors. During the day, those doors framed a perfect view of the Chesapeake Bay, but at night I wondered who might be out there. I turned off the light and watched the blue flames flicker on the stovetop. When the kettle hissed, I flinched again. My heart raced, reminding me how Coach Kent had whistled a cocky little tune as he followed too close behind me on the stairs to my father-in-law's conference room.

It began last fall, shortly after he chose my daughter, Amber, to be on the varsity sailing team. He knew I wouldn't do anything to jeopardize her chance at a college sailing scholarship. Late one night, on the way home from a regatta I was chaperoning, he stopped the van at a Krispy Kreme. As the teens spilled out to run inside, he slid his hand up my blouse. I froze, trapped by the fear of making a scene in front of my daughter and her friends. Once they had all disappeared inside the store, I clamped my hand on his and wriggled out, telling him firmly to stop. When the kids returned, he reached for me again, knowing I would stay quiet. Sometimes he sent dick pics afterward with the note, "Thinking of you."

I was enraged with myself for acting so perky after it happened again yesterday. My father-in-law left us alone together in his conference room while he prepared a check for the unveiling celebration. Coach Kent grabbed me between my legs, pinning me against the heavy, wooden law office doors. When Dwight Sr. returned, I laughed nervously like nothing had happened. I took the check and slipped out as he and Coach Kent sat down to discuss the order of events for the ceremony.

If I blew the whistle, would my daughter believe I hadn't invited the coach's attention? She hero-worshiped him and, I suspected, also had a huge crush. I told myself to forget about it. Today was his last day in Mobjack.

As the sailing team's communications mom, I often composed my text blasts in the early hours when I couldn't sleep—but I never allowed myself to press "send" before seven o'clock.

Good morning, everyone!
Join us today at 10:00
for the unveiling of our sailing champions' mural
and to wish Coach Kent farewell
Cookies and punch to follow on the Village Green!

I forgot my rule and, *bwoop,* sent it to everyone at 3:37 a.m. Realizing it a second too late, I threw my phone across the room into the couch. After fishing it out of the crack in the cushions, I buried my face in a throw pillow and drifted off.

Summer solstice rays jolted me awake. I would be late for work if I didn't hurry. Passing Amber's bedroom at the top of the stairs, I caught sight of her America's Cup poster signed by Coach Kent, surrounded by sailing trophies and colorful burgees from yacht clubs where she and her teammates had competed.

Before Amber's senior year, she had been a quiet loner without many friends or interests. At sixteen, she spent her free time in our neighbor's yard, playing with their neglected farm animals. When my ex-husband, Dwight, would try to talk to her about colleges, Amber would remind us, "College isn't for everyone, ya know."

Amber's life changed overnight when Coach Kent recognized the skipper in her. Her confidence snapped open like a billowing spinnaker. After winning her first regatta, she burst into our bedroom with the news, "Coach Kent thinks I might be a good candidate for a sailing scholarship to college." Elated by our daughter's new spirit, Dwight and I had sex that night for the first time in forever. But it wasn't enough to save our marriage.

I rushed through the shower without waiting for the water to get hot. Sifting through the dresses in my closet, I searched for something nice to wear for today's events. Not too dressy, but a step up from my usual black jeans. In my hurry, I jabbed myself in the eye with my liquid eyeliner brush, making one of my blue eyes secrete thick black tears.

* * *

I began punching in the café's alarm code before I discovered it wasn't armed. The oily aroma of flavored coffees—hazelnut, French vanilla, and Irish cream—had seeped into the old wooden floors and beams of the Slack Tide Café in the short time since our grand opening. As I moved around the room counterclockwise to turn on the lamps, I detected a cigarette burning in the back room.

"Another fight with your girlfriend?" I called to Sylvia from behind the register, where I saw she had already completed the crossword puzzle.

She pushed open the wooden swing door with her hip, holding the stray cat I had told her to stop feeding. "Nah. Full moon." When Sylvia was upset, she would sometimes paint all night at her easel under the high-wattage fluorescent lighting in the back room of the café. She put the cat down, turned on the vacuum, and began running it around the seating area.

I started making coffee and filling the milk containers, hollering over the noise of the vacuum and the coffee grinder. "You could've come over to my place—I was awake most of the night too."

Swing Bridge

She yanked the vacuum cord to kill the noise and flopped in one of the overstuffed armchairs. "Claire, you're gonna be really pissed at me this time."

I dropped the bean scoop and wiped the coffee grinds on my apron. Sylvia was my best friend, but she could be unpredictable and impulsive. Like last fall. When we arrived at the Mobjack Invitational Regatta, she insisted that the blonde standing next to my husband was the woman she had seen him having an affair with. A little drunk on mimosas after a gallery opening, Sylvia dismissed my protests and made a scene in front of all the other parents. As it turned out, the woman was just a client. I could have killed Sylvia, but her good heart and deep loyalty always made me forgive her. Dwight Jr. *was* having an affair—but not with *that* woman.

I took off my grimy apron as she loosened another cigarette from the pack in her oversized, paint-covered smock. "If you're going to smoke," I said, pulling her to her feet, "let's go out back."

Outside, she sat on one of the concrete steps next to the walk-in fridge, between the recycling bins, scooting to one side so I could join her. I shook my head, not wanting to get my linen dress dirty.

"So what's going on?" I coaxed, mindful that we only had a few minutes before the morning rush. Strains of heavy metal music came from the auto-repair shop next door, where Benny started work every morning at six, waiting until eight to be our first customer.

"Today's the unveiling," she whined, playing with the laces on her paint-splattered Doc Martens.

I put my hands on my hips and stared down at her. So talented and creative, she had easily won the design contest for the three-story mosaic mural celebrating Mobjack's sailing team winning the national championship. "It's not like you to worry about what other people think," I prodded, impatient to know what was wrong.

"I'm worried you'll be pissed because the mural they're going to unveil isn't based on the approved design."

"Excuse me?"

My father-in-law, Dwight Sr., had converted the former department store in the center of town into office space to house his growing law firm. As a favor to his granddaughter, he agreed to let the sailing team put a mural on his building with one condition: He had to approve the design. Sylvia's profile of Coach Kent with a line of triumphant sailboats in the distance met with Dwight Sr.'s conservative approval. Everyone contributed broken pottery, tile, mirror shards, and ceramics, along with locally abundant materials like piles of oyster shells and colorful sea glass. When the scaffolding came down, an enormous drop cloth hung from the roof of Dwight Sr.'s building, concealing the mural for today's ceremony.

Sylvia ran her hand through her salt-and-pepper shag-cut before looking up at me. "I altered the design when I made the template. That's why I insisted on keeping the project tightly veiled until today."

"Oh my God, Syl, *what's* on that wall?" I squeezed my temples, imagining the worst.

Benny cleared his throat from the doorway. "Can I get some service here?"

Sylvia jumped up. "Benny, we've told you not to go behind the counter. You're supposed to ring the bell if we're not there." She never liked for anyone to see her unfinished paintings.

* * *

Swing Bridge

Our morning rush was busier than usual with everyone coming into town to say goodbye to Coach Kent.

A year ago, he arrived in Mobjack by boat to open a sales office for an international yacht company to cover the Tidewater region of Virginia. Today, he planned to sail away after the ceremony to open another sales office across the Bay. When he arrived, the *Mobjack Mirror* printed an interview with him where he described his experience crewing for Team USA in the America's Cup. When he heard our small public school had no varsity sailing team, he offered to help us form one.

"Hell yeah, we're going to win the Baker Trophy," he had bragged to a group of excited parents. "I only coach champions."

His company donated a fleet of international 420 class dinghies. Unlike most high school sports, interscholastic sailing was coed. As our kids competed to make the team, the parents vied for opportunities to chaperone.

While Sylvia and I served a steady stream of customers, I grew more worried about what Sylvia had put on that wall. After the rush died down, my father-in-law stopped by on his way to the office. Reflexively, I made his caramel macchiato and used tongs to place a blueberry scone on a plate.

"Mornin', Dad," I called over my shoulder as I steamed his almond milk. I still called him Dad, even though my divorce was almost final. Sylvia thought he looked like Andy Warhol with crazy white hair and vintage sunglasses, a high compliment coming from her. I admired him too. Dwight Sr. was kind, gentle, and honest—nothing like his foul-tempered, lying, cheater of a son. I don't know what I would have done without his support throughout the divorce.

"Thank you, dear," Dwight Sr. said, taking his coffee drink and scone from the counter. With a tilt of his head, he signaled he wanted to talk to me.

I blushed, wondering if he somehow knew what happened in his conference room yesterday. Or had he peeked at Sylvia's unapproved mural? Struggling to seem casual, I removed my apron and asked, "Should I bring the expense report?"

After Dwight Jr.'s midlife crisis ruined our marriage, my father-in-law stepped in to take care of Amber and me financially. To get me out of the house, he hired me to be a legal secretary in his estate planning law firm, but after a week, he could tell office work wasn't for me.

"What do you think you *would* like to do," he had asked.

My reply that I enjoyed interior decorating gave him an idea. His firm would buy the country store across the street from his office and let me fix it up as a coffee shop. He assured me the café didn't have to make a profit because his law partners planned to "use the losses to offset some gains," creating dream jobs for Sylvia and me.

"No, don't bother with the report. I just want to know how you're doing. I worry about you in that big house by yourself."

"I'm okay, Dad. Thanks for asking. When the divorce is finalized, I'll sell it and find something smaller."

Dwight Sr.'s mouth was full, so he nodded. After a pause, he asked, "Has Amber started speaking to you again?"

My eyes filled with tears as I shook my head.

"I'm sorry I brought it up. She'll come around soon, don't you worry."

When Dwight Jr's affair came to light last fall, Sylvia offered to let Amber stay with her. At the time, I thought it was a good idea.

I wanted to spare Amber the ugliness of our fighting. But I soon regretted it. Amber was so angry at Dwight and me when we told her we were divorcing that she stopped speaking to both of us. From then on, she confided in Sylvia the things she used to share with me.

Dwight Sr. wiped the crumbs from his mouth and looked at his watch. "Not long now." He pointed outside at the volunteers setting up for the ceremony. On his way out, he hollered over his shoulder toward the back room, "Big day, Sylvia—bet you're anxious to see how your work looks three stories high." Without waiting for her response, he strode through the door saying, "Put it on my tab." He cracked himself up since he owned the place and didn't have a tab.

My stomach tightened at Dwight Sr.'s mention of the unveiling. I found Sylvia in the back room spreading a thick layer of red paint across her canvas with the blade of her Swiss Army Knife, like she was frosting a cake. As I drew in a breath to ask again what was on that wall, the phone in her paint smock rang—Amber's ringtone.

Sylvia held up her paint-covered hands. "Put her on speaker."

I removed the phone from her smock and placed it on one of the jugs of pink hand soap for the bathroom dispenser.

"What's up, Amber?" Sylvia said.

"Hey. Can I invite the team for a sleepover at your place tonight after Coach Kent leaves? They'll bring sleeping bags—I promise we'll keep the noise down."

Sylvia looked at me with widening eyes. "You know, your mom has a *huge* house where you and your friends could spread out—maybe even have a cookout?"

"Nice try, Sylvia. Is she standing right there?"

I appreciated Sylvia's attempts to help us reconcile, but I knew Amber wouldn't come around until she was ready. Leaving them to negotiate a sleepover, I busied myself by watering the plant in the front window.

Outside, a crowd was gathering in the intersection. The sheriff's deputies were blocking off the road to traffic, and a fire engine was positioned with its ladder extended so Tracy, one of the volunteer firefighters, could remove the cloth at the designated time.

A reporter from the *Mobjack Mirror* popped her head in to see if Sylvia would give her a comment before the unveiling.

"She's on the phone," I said, flipping the "open" sign to "closed," and locking the door behind her.

When Sylvia finished her call, I sat her down on one of the stools at the coffee bar. Folding my arms, I said, "We're not going anywhere until you tell me what's on that wall."

She looked away from me and sighed. "My silent protest."

"That's what I was afraid of." I stomped my leather sandal on the wide floorboard. "You shouldn't have done that."

"I know it was supposed to be a tribute to him, but the way he's harassed you makes me sick. You swore me to secrecy—and I haven't told a soul—but I couldn't stand creating art that would honor him. He'll be gone, but *we'll* have to look at that wall every day for the rest of our lives."

"You could have at least discussed it with me and shown me your *alternate* design."

"Be real, Claire. You never would have agreed to let me make protest art on your father-in-law's building."

With tears of rage surfacing, I said, "You have to stop fighting my battles for me."

She slid off the stool. "Wait, Claire, I'm sorry I—" She tried to give me a hug, but I pushed her away with the force I should have used on Coach Kent in the conference room.

Outside, my father-in-law's voice came over a loudspeaker, asking for everyone's attention. I smoothed the wrinkles in my dress, unlocked the door, and stood on the porch of the café to watch the proceedings from behind the crowd.

Coach Kent approached the microphone. Like a rock star, he had to wait for the crowd to stop whistling and whooping before he could speak. He looked tan and athletic in shorts and a polo with sun streaks in his wavy golden hair. I remembered the smell of his breath and felt a wave of nausea.

"And now…" Coach Kent was trying to settle the crowd, but the audience only got louder. He tapped the toe of his Top-Sider against the pavement like a bashful little boy. I caught sight of Amber in the crowd, her arms raised overhead, clapping.

"And now for the—" More cheering. While he waited for the ovation to subside, he pointed at individuals in the crowd, mugging for their cameras from the podium.

"And now for the moment we've all been waiting for." He motioned to Tracy in the fire truck bucket to remove the cloth.

It took a while for Tracy to unhook each grommet from the top of the building. The crowd tilted their heads back, shading their eyes from the late morning sun.

As I waited with the crowd, my fingers curled around the phone in my pocket, fumbling with urgency. Before I knew it, I had found one of Coach Kent's dick pics and prepared a text-blast to send to the sailing community standing before me. I added the note, "Coach Kent sexually harassed me all year."

Bwoop.

The cloth fell from the roof, but on the way down, it snagged on one of the protruding objects in the mosaic—a teapot spout. We all craned our necks to watch the aerial ladder lower Tracy to the problem area.

Everyone's phone pinged.

I froze.

Some people glanced down, but most waited to see the mural. Tracy stretched dangerously outside of the bucket to unsnag the cloth, but it caught *again* on an angel's wing farther down— a broken Christmas tree ornament. Annoyed by the delays, more people looked at their phones. By the time the canvas snagged a third time, everyone was staring at their phones.

Some kids snickered, while others looked confused. Parents and teachers covered their mouths, embarrassed.

Another ping chimed from everyone's phones—mine too this time. I glanced down at my phone to find another Coach Kent dick pic—this one sent by one of the other sailing moms with the note, "ME TOO."

Five more dick pics followed in rapid succession from five other sailing moms. The crowd had completely forgotten about the mural. Murmurs turned to shouting with everyone demanding an explanation from Coach Kent. As he tried to escape, two of the sheriff's deputies who had been blocking traffic pursued him on foot. The crowd, including Sylvia, swarmed behind to see what would happen.

I watched as the fire truck ladder retracted and Tracy ran to catch up with the crowd.

Alone beneath the mural, I sat in a rocking chair on the café porch and gazed at the fully unveiled mosaic. The simplicity surprised me. A single sailboat struggled to remain upright at the base of a tidal wave cresting ominously above. Shards of mirror caught the light at different angles, sparkling like sunlight on water. Small and vulnerable, the rickety copper hull clung to the trough of the wave, beneath the towering swell, propelled by the forceful motion threatening it. At the top, the words *Sail Forth* slanted forward in a handwritten script, as if the wind were blowing the wave, the boat, and all of us into the future.

The Bel-Mar Blade

MY OLDER SISTER BLASTED back into our lives as if no time had passed. Belle hadn't returned to the Island in almost eight years, not since I refused to be her maid of honor and Mumma and Fletch refused to let her have her big day under the willow oak. Naturally, she had to show up now to ruin *my* big plans.

"Bring Fletch's truck," Belle texted. "My Corvette's in the ditch by the cemetery."

The Bel-Mar blade in the news must have called her home. When we were babies our daddy, Fletch, captained a fishing boat that trawled for sea scallops in the lower part of the Chesapeake. One day he and his crew dredged up part of a mastodon skull with a nine-inch stone blade embedded in it. Fletch called it the Bel-Mar blade after his workboat, the *Bel-Mar*, which he named after my sister, Belle, and me, Maren.

"Can't," I texted back. "On my way to see Pastor Polly."

"Don't tell me you found Jesus since I've been away!"

"None of your business. What are you doing here?"

"Just send Fletch."

Fletch wasn't available either. He drove to Washington this morning to retrieve the Bel-Mar blade from the Smithsonian after they radiocarbon dated it. Fletch hated the city. He would rant about the one-way streets, parallel parking, and how city folk couldn't understand his Tidewater accent, making him repeat himself like a foreigner.

"Then *you'll* have to come."

"Is Troy with you?"

"No."

"On my way."

I texted Polly to ask if I could come over later. Wednesday afternoons were the only times Polly would allow me to see her. At least until the rumors died down.

"Bitch in a ditch ☺," Polly texted back.

Growing up, Belle would make me stay home with Mumma so she could go to parties off the Island. Mumma was wheelchair-bound from a boating accident before we were born, which left her paralyzed from the waist down. We always had to explain that yes, paralyzed people can have sex and give birth. The liquor store on the mainland delivered cases of gin and cartons of cigarettes to our house every week. Belle wasn't popular but she was invited to every high school party to bring the booze. I never smoked or drank, but Belle took right after Mumma. We both wanted to escape the Island more than anything, but Mumma always said one of us would have to stay to take care of her and the farm so Fletch could work. I couldn't compete with Belle. She was a year older and willing to do *anything* to get away.

When I pulled up by the cemetery in Fletch's Ram, I recognized Belle from behind. She stood on a gravestone, yelling into her phone—probably at Troy, her fish-faced husband. Even though she had changed her hair from straight and mousy-brown like mine to a bushy blond perm, her hand-on-hip pose with the opposite toe pointing up reminded me of her bossy temper. A floral-print romper hid the weight she had gained.

Running my finger along the damage, I wondered how Belle fit in the thing. She had scraped and dented the entire right side by plowing through the underbrush. Helpless little red Corvette.

As I lay on my back in the ditch hooking the chain to her axle, something yipped from inside the car. Wiping pine tags off my softball jersey, I peered inside. A tiny dog was shaking in Belle's purse on the passenger seat. Belle snuck up from behind and gave me a bear hug that felt more like the Heimlich maneuver, lifting me off the ground.

Belle had always enjoyed doing this, making me kick and scream. Six feet tall and overweight, she could lift an astonishing amount. She took after Mumma while I resembled Fletch, small and lean.

"Put me down, Belle," I demanded. "I'm trying to do *you* a favor."

She released me with a phlegmy smoker's laugh. "Did you meet Chloe?"

"Not exactly. Why's she shaking?"

"Separation anxiety. Don't judge. She takes medication for it."

Belle popped open the trunk and began sorting through samples of wild-print leggings until she found a pair patterned with Ruth Bader Ginsberg's face.

"These retail for twenty but since they're perfect for you, I'll let 'em go for eighteen."

"No, thanks." I pivoted toward the Ram to retract the winch.

"When you see how much I make selling these, give me a call," she said, slamming the trunk. "I might have an opportunity for you."

"Put the car in neutral," I ordered over my shoulder.

* * *

When we arrived at the farmhouse, Fletch's hunting dogs—thirteen beagles with numbers spray-painted on their sides—howled and barked from their pen, alerting Mumma to look through her peephole. Fletch had installed it at chair level in their bedroom on the ground floor so she could decide whether or not to answer the door when he was away fishing.

Belle stood in the driveway, striking her hip-and-toe pose. "It looks smaller than I remember," she said, looking up at her old bedroom window. Waiting for Mumma to come out, she drifted toward the swing hanging from the willow oak overlooking the back side of Fletch's boathouse on the creek.

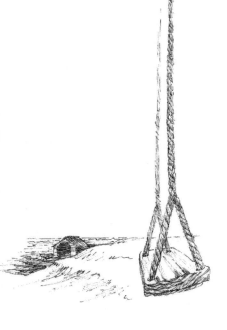

I hadn't missed Belle. I wished it had been me who got away. Mumma and Fletch did too, I think. I was afraid Mumma would drink more than ever after Belle left, but instead she stopped drinking, settling into a permanent bad mood. As she and Fletch argued through holidays—and even big events like when Neil Diamond performed "Sweet Caroline" at the high school—I felt Belle's absence the most. Whether I liked it or not, we needed Belle's craziness for balance.

Everyone always said *I* should be the one to leave the Island after high school. I made good grades and wanted to go to college. Belle dropped out when she landed a decent-paying job in the office of the marina during her senior year. That's how she met Troy, a marine surveyor from the city. He was forty-three and Belle was eighteen. To me, he resembled the lumpfish we were dissecting in biology class—the back of his crew cut flat, and his eyes bulging too far apart. But to Belle, he was beautiful because he had a lot of money. According to Fletch, he had too much money for a marine surveyor.

Soon after Belle met Troy, she dragged me to a party at his house in the city. I didn't want to tag along, but Fletch said Belle couldn't go alone. I was scared to go inside because one of Troy's skinhead friends was shooting at empty tequila bottles on the porch with a BB gun. Belle fit right in, a pro at drinking shots and shooting darts. I motioned to her that I'd be upstairs until she was ready to go. In the bathroom there was a pile of porno magazines. Even though they were disgusting, I couldn't help flipping through them. When Troy busted in by accident, he ran back downstairs shouting that I was a horny little dyke. "That's it." I handed Belle her purse, but she kept tugging at my arm to sing karaoke with her. I ended up hiding in Fletch's truck until two in the morning when Belle was finally ready to leave. The whole ride home she was pissed at *me* for offending her boyfriend.

At the end of the summer, Belle quit her job at the marina, announcing she and Troy were engaged. She had the nerve to ask me to be her maid of honor. "Are you crazy?" I shouted. "I don't ever want to be in the same room with him again." Unphased, she turned to Fletch to ask if she could have her ceremony under the willow oak. Fletch said no. He didn't trust Troy. Mumma was her last hope. Belle kneeled in front of her asking for her blessing but Mumma stayed silent, her gaze fixed on the burn pile where last week's trash was smoldering. Belle sprang into a rage, swearing she'd never speak to any of us again.

When Belle heard Mumma trying to open the front door with her grabby stick, she hurried back to her car to cradle her dog. As Mumma wheeled across the threshold onto the porch, Belle dropped the dog and ran to her.

I slipped down to the boathouse to check in with Polly. Mumma's and Belle's laughter rang across the creek, reminding me of how Mumma used to do doughnuts on the porch with Belle draped across her lap.

I texted Polly: "Would it ever occur to Mumma that *I'm* to thank for Belle coming home? If I hadn't contacted that archeologist, she wouldn't be here now."

Stuck on the Island long after everyone my age had gone, searching for something to do, I wondered about the history of the Bel-Mar blade. Our family had always treasured it as a souvenir, believing it carried good luck, but I figured maybe it had scientific importance too. In my letter to Virginia's leading expert in paleolithic projectile points, I explained where and how the Bel-Mar blade was found, enclosing a nautical chart with the GPS location, measurements, and several photos. To my surprise, he called right away.

Fletch had tensed when I told him a scientist was coming to see the blade. Normally, he would get rid of come-heres by filibustering on Chesapeake Bay fishing conditions until their patience timed out, so I grabbed my archeologist in the driveway and led him down to the boathouse. We weighed the blade and I helped him use a portable scanner to determine if there was enough organic material from the mastodon skull to radiocarbon date it. When we got a positive reading, we were both super excited. He suggested I send the blade to the Smithsonian's forensic analysis lab, saying we might have a major find. As he was leaving, he handed me his card. "Call me if you'd like a job."

"Thanks, but," I nodded toward the house, "I'm kind of stuck here."

No sooner had I FedExed the blade to Washington than Fletch regretted signing the permission papers. The radiocarbon dating didn't take long—a few days. What took so long was the scientists fighting among themselves about how to report the significance of the results: The Bel-Mar blade turned out to be twenty-three thousand years old. Prior to this the oldest known artifact from the Americas was only thirteen thousand years old, brought by the Clovis people across the frozen Bering Strait from Siberia to Alaska during the ice age. The Bel-Mar blade supported an alternative theory that the Solutreans, who lived in the area where Spain was today, traveled across the edge of the Atlantic shelf. The longer shape of the Bel-Mar blade matched the Solutrean style, indicating that the first people here may have come from Europe, not Asia. Most scientists regarded the Solutrean hypothesis as a wishful White supremacist theory, but the Bel-Mar blade's age gave them all pause. Eventually they concluded that one artifact wasn't enough evidence to overturn decades of research.

When the Smithsonian finally announced their findings in a press release last week, a news crew came to interview me and Fletch. Fletch described the day of discovery, and I described my plans to convert Fletch's boathouse into a floating museum where people could arrive

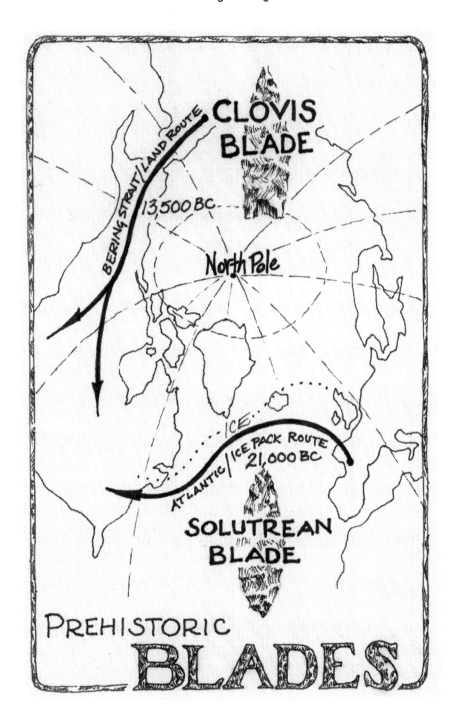

by boat to see the mastodon skull, the Bel-Mar blade, and the old wooden trawler that dredged them up.

Polly texted back, "Do U know the parable of the prodigal son?"

Before I could tell her to spare me the sermon, the hunting dogs went crazy. I bolted up the lawn, hoping it was Fletch, home with the Bel-Mar blade.

I stopped short. Fletch and Belle were locked in a stand-off I knew not to interrupt. Belle had an apologetic look, but Fletch was hard to read. Mumma stopped laughing, frozen on the porch. Even the dogs quit barking. Fletch's face relaxed into a huge smile, and he stretched out his arms. As Belle bounded toward him, the dogs resumed barking, and Mumma went back to laughing.

I removed a rectangular package the size of a candy box from Fletch's satchel and ran my finger over the embossed label: Smithsonian Institution, Natural History Museum, Department of Forensic Analysis. Lifting it to my nose, I detected battery acid and a hint of coffee.

"Hallelujah!" I shouted. "The Bel-Mar blade is home!"

Mumma and Fletch erupted in laughter over something Belle said.

Carrying the sealed box in front of me like a sacred relic, I followed them inside so we could open it together, but Belle had already whipped out her phone and was showing Mumma and Fletch pictures of her glam life.

"Look at Troy's catamaran!" Mumma exclaimed. "It must be—"

"—yes, Mumma, sixty feet!" Belle beamed. "We hire a private yacht chef when we go to the Bahamas."

I studied Fletch to see if he was impressed. He seemed genuinely interested, holding Belle's little dog, petting its head, leaning over Mumma to see the pictures.

"Maren, please put dinner on," Mumma said. "Get out the good china, and how 'bout you fry up those oysters you shucked yesterday?"

Banished to the kitchen, I resented Mumma for not even looking at me from her wheelchair throne. Waiting for the grease in the frypan to heat, I strained to overhear their conversation.

Mumma, Fletch, and I had stopped eating meals together after Belle left. As we took our former seats, Mumma reached for our hands. With a bowed head, she raised her eyes to Fletch, who said the fisherman's prayer for the first time in eight years.

After everyone served themselves, Belle got to the point. "So what are we going to do with the Bel-Mar blade? Troy knows somebody who wants to buy it for ten thousand dollars."

"It's not for sale," I said, my eyes searching Fletch's for assurance. "It's going to be the main attraction of my museum."

"Ten thousand dollars?" Mumma whistled through her teeth.

"I don't know if we should sell it," Fletch said. "The Bel-Mar blade has always brought us good luck. See how it answered our prayers?" He and Mumma beamed at Belle.

Tilting her head back to poke an oyster into her surprisingly small mouth, Belle said, "We need to sell the blade while the alternative theory is hot, if you know what I mean." A stream of oyster juice squirted across the table when she bit down.

"That's disgusting, Belle," I cried. "You're proud of the fact that Troy and his friends are White supremacists?"

"I didn't say proud. I said we should sell it to them while they're interested. I might be able to get them to go up to fifteen thousand if we had another bidder. How much will the Smithsonian give us?"

"Nothing," Fletch said. "The know-it-alls in Washington can only take stuff that's donated."

"Who cares what race arrived here first?" Mumma said. "They were all cavemen."

"Paleo-Indians," I corrected.

"Well, I'm trying to launch my leggings business, and I could use some start-up cash," Belle said.

We all stopped chewing.

She burst into tears, putting her forehead on the table so we couldn't see her face. "Troy's in jail, arrested for drug smuggling. All of his bank accounts are frozen. Go on, tell me you told me so."

After a brief pause Mumma said, "That's wonderful news! You can get your job back at the marina."

"What?" I felt like I was going crazy. "That's my job now. You think I should give it back after all these years because her husband's in jail?"

"Relax, Maren," Belle said, blowing her nose into her cloth napkin. "I don't want that stupid job back. I want to sell the Bel-Mar blade so I can use my half to get my leggings business off the ground. I need five thousand dollars for my inventory and marketing materials."

"Sounds like a pyramid scheme," Fletch muttered.

"The leggings *are* cute," Mumma said, already wearing a pair.

"No way." I turned to Fletch. "I finally get a chance to do something with my life besides wait on Mumma, and just as I'm about to open my waterfront museum, Belle shows up wanting to *sell* my exhibit?" I left the table with the Smithsonian box tucked under my elbow, dropped my plate in the sink, and slammed out the kitchen door to be alone on the dock.

The yolk-like September sun was sinking behind pine trees across the creek. I texted Polly: "Really need to see you. Can I come over?"

"Maybe after the ladies sorting clothes for the fall fair go home."

Swing Bridge

Mosquitos feasted on my ankles as I composed a text to Polly, telling her how much I hated the way she treated me. When the last of the yolk drained away, Belle snuck up from behind and lifted me in the air again. "Who's Polly? Your girlfriend?"

"None of your business."

"Have you come out to Mumma and Fletch yet?"

I started to deny I was gay out of habit, then gave up. "If you must know, we can't tell anyone because Polly's afraid she'll lose her pastor job."

She raised an eyebrow before changing the subject. "Let's see your museum." Belle threw open one of the two doors to Fletch's boathouse.

I turned on the overhead light and followed her to the wooden case Fletch and I had made to display our projectile when it returned from Washington.

"Looks like a coffin for a baby," she said.

"Visitors will enter the museum over there." I pointed to the opposite corner. "They'll start the tour by boarding the *Bel-Mar*'s bow. When they step off the stern, they'll wait in line to see the skull behind the curtain in that corner. Then they'll follow this rope barrier to take turns viewing the main exhibit in this case, exiting by the door we just came in."

"No gift shop?" She cracked herself up. "I bet I could sell your visitors some leggings."

Insulted, I walked over to the light switch, threatening to leave her alone in the dark.

A wave of excitement came over Belle's piggy face. "I've got it. We'll sell the Bel-Mar blade and make a *replica* for your exhibit—Troy knows a guy who can make *anything*."

"Nice try, Belle. We're not going to sell the Bel-Mar blade."

The Bel-Mar Blade

"Who would know the difference?"

"*I'll* know the difference. I can't *knowingly* display a fake artifact."

"Why not?" Belle asked, lighting a cigarette. "Aren't you living a lie by not telling Mumma and Fletch you're gay?"

"Go *outside* to smoke," I yelled, pushing her big butt out the door.

I expected her to shove her way back in or come around to the other door. Instead she beelined up the hill, on fire with purpose. My panic surged. I feared she was either going to out me to Mumma and Fletch or convince them to sell the Bel-Mar blade, promising to give me a replica for my museum. Maybe both. Mumma and Fletch—so thrilled to have her home—wouldn't dare cross her again.

I imagined what it would feel like to hurl the Bel-Mar blade as far as I could into the creek, letting it settle among the fossils buried in the eel grass for another thousand years so neither of us could have it. Using my Swiss Army Knife, I broke the seal on the Smithsonian box, pried off the top, and read the letter of authentication. My fingertips measured the blade's familiar weight. Balancing it by the ends, I held it under the light to confirm that half was darker from being buried in the mastodon skull and the other half was lighter from Belle and me rubbing it for good luck. Satisfied it was no fake, I opened the display case and placed the Bel-Mar blade on the black velvet cushion. After rubbing the light end one more time, I closed the case.

When I turned off the boathouse light, bioluminescent algae glowed green around the *Bel-Mar*'s stern as water lapped the barnacle-covered pilings.

Staring into the water, I dredged up a fragment of hope. With Belle home to care for Mumma, I wasn't stuck anymore.

I checked my wallet to see if I still had the archeologist's card. Before I could change my mind, I texted Polly to break it off.

Swing Bridge

My headlights illuminated the curve at the cemetery. With laser focus on the road ahead, I slowed way down, tightening my grip on the wheel. No way was I going to slip into that ditch.

Hurricane Hole

J IMMY WARNED ME we might lose contact during the hurricane, so it was important to stick to the plan: meet at the Harborside Motel & Marina in Key West as soon as the money hit my account.

I waited on the porch in Mobjack, Virginia, wearing my midlife uniform: a flannel shirt over jeans and Crocs, and—my signature feature—long, curly blonde hair with highlights, wild and loose. Right on time, a silver Lexus pulled into my drive. This angel of a woman had purchased my house and business, sight unseen, freeing me to start my new life with Jimmy. I was in a hurry to complete the sale, but curious to meet her in person.

I couldn't see through the tinted windows of her car. When the car door opened, a pointy black heel pierced the gravel. My eyes traveled up a white pantsuit, pausing to note gold jewelry on her wrists, neck, and ears before our sunglasses met.

"I tried to hide my shock. "I thought you were a Toli—"

"You didn't expect me to be Black, did you?" With folded arms, she waited for me to remember there were Black Tolivers too, descendants from the enslaved people on the Toliver plantation. She stretched out her soft, manicured hand. "Hello, White Judy. I'm Black Judy."

* * *

Jimmy captained a forty-two-foot sloop made of Honduran mahogany, varnished to perfection. He made his money buying old wooden boats, fixing them up to sell. The first time we met, his antique yacht had drawn a crowd at Whitman's Marina on Wynn's Island. His eyes bounced like skipping stones, selecting *me* to come aboard for dock-tails. A few hours later, squinting across the bay, he looked so vulnerable. "I have a great life—living on the water, working for myself—but I'm lonely." I was lonely too, ever since my son left home seven years ago. I would have sailed away with him that night before he even kissed me, but I couldn't abandon my home and business.

It turned out to be harder than I expected to find a buyer. My home and business were combined, zoned residential *and* commercial. Lots of people wanted my business, but nobody wanted to *live* on a toilet rental farm.

I had always imagined my son would take it over one day. He dropped out of grad school to move in with his professor, helping her with some sort of tech start-up. She was almost my age, but I don't judge.

"Mom, are you high?" That's how he spoke to me. "I'm twenty-five, making six figures, and you want me to run your porta-potty business?"

He was too young to appreciate how business on Wynn's Island wasn't only about money. "It's also about community—like how my business sponsored your robotics team every year."

"I'll help you post it on Craigslist," he said, explaining that's how I could avoid paying a broker's commission.

After dropping the price a third time, I finally found a buyer last week. I called Jimmy on the boat. "The sale is happening real fast, not full price but all cash. Are you sure you still want me? I mean for your business partner?"

Jimmy and I had a plan to offer sunset cruises together. He would be the captain, of course, and I would be the hostess, serving customers drinks and snacks. He said my cheesy spinach dip and pretty smile would get us good tips and reviews.

"Fly down to Key West after the hurricane passes," he instructed. "I'll pick you up at Harborside. Remember—you can't bring too much onboard. Two small bags, max."

I didn't even need two bags for my summer clothes, bathing suit, hair gel, and Swiss Army Knife. I dropped all my winter clothes at Goodwill months ago when we first hatched the plan.

I had called Judy to see if we could finalize our deal before the storm hit Mobjack. "Hurricanes are great for potty rentals," I pointed out. "Lots of repair business afterwards. You'll see—your phone will ring off the hook with contractors needing you to deliver potties to their construction sites."

She agreed to meet the next morning. If everything looked good, I would hand her the keys, and she would drive me to the airport in Richmond, since my truck was part of the deal.

* * *

Self-conscious about my calloused hands and nubby fingernails, I let go of Judy's hand with an awkward smile. I showed her around the property, pointing out the generator, septic field, and pump-out truck. When we got to the potty barn—my storage facility pieced together from scrap metal like an airplane hangar—she inspected each potty. Our contract specified a hundred and fifty potties and twenty sinks. The slow tick tock of her heels on the concrete floor made me anxious. While she inventoried, I slipped outside to call my son.

"She's Black," I whispered.

"Mom, I keep telling you—you've got to check your racism. Remember how we talked about—"

"Yeah, yeah, I gotta go." I hung up and tiptoed back inside. Judy had discovered that eleven potties and three sinks were missing.

"They're not missing," I said. "They're on job sites making you money."

She folded her arms and raised an eyebrow. "When were you going to share this information with me? Where are these job sites?"

Judy's lawyer had written a contract that I signed on my phone, just like that. Then boom. She wired the deposit into my account yesterday, pointing out the one contingency: when she got to Mobjack, all the assets had to be on the premises, with no liens. I never had any debt, if that's what she meant.

I apologized for forgetting to mention the job sites, explaining how distracted I had been, unable to reach Jimmy in the Caribbean. "My boyfriend anchored in a hurricane hole somewhere near the British Virgin Islands. I begged him not to stay on his boat during the storm, but he said the water was the safest place to ride it out. That was three days ago. Not a word from him since."

Judy nodded. Then she asked to see my financials.

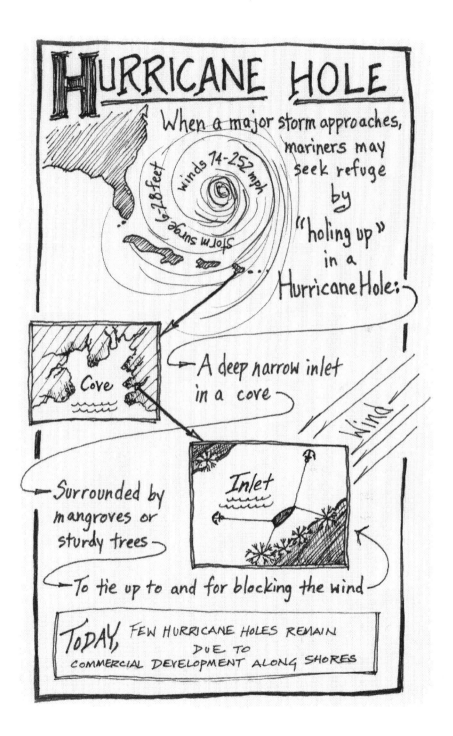

"Do you mean my notebook?" It was one of those black-and-white composition books you buy at the dollar store. I kept a running list of my potty sites and delivery dates so I could invoice for the right number of days.

Stepping back outside, Judy looked at me from over her sunglasses. "This is your accounting system?"

She had sounded so nice over the phone, but she was starting to get on my nerves. Two weeks ago, she'd called from Richmond—only two hours away—saying she was interested in buying my property. Said her name was Judy too, which was perfect because she wouldn't have to change the branding. When she asked for my bank account and routing numbers so she could wire the money, I flipped out. "Is this some sort of scam?"

She'd explained that she was looking for an income-generating business in the Tidewater area because she wanted to move back to Mobjack, where her family was from. When she came across Judy's Toilet Rentals, she figured it was meant to be.

"Really, your people are here? What's the last name?"

Everyone knew everyone in Mobjack, so this was the best reference check. The name she gave me, Toliver, was one of the oldest, most respected names, so I figured she was legit. Our cemetery was full of Tolivers, going back to the 1600s.

When I told Judy I needed time to sell my furniture, she said she'd buy it. I was thrilled because I wanted to start my life with Jimmy ASAP.

Judy started questioning me about where I kept my depreciation schedules. To my relief, Dr. Bozwell drove up in the Rescue Squad truck. He was the evacuation coordinator for Mobjack County.

Leaning out his open window, he said, "Don't make me carry you off the island, Judy. This storm is moving faster than predicted—and it's more powerful than anything we've seen in decades. Nothing to play around with. You and your guest need to leave right now before the swing bridge closes."

"Boz, this is Judy Toliver. She's buying my business."

Boz nodded, welcoming her to Mobjack.

"Which one of you owns the business right now?" he asked.

"She does," we both said at the same time.

"Have you corralled your potties?" His head swiveled between me and her. "You know what happens." He fixed his gaze on me.

"No, what happens?" Judy asked.

"Oh lordy," Boz exclaimed. "When a big storm hits, the potties fly all across the bay."

"Shut. Up," I mouthed behind Judy's back. But Boz continued.

"Remember how the Squad helped you collect them from as far away as Cape Charles?"

"Oh yeah." I forced a chuckle.

Judy was not laughing.

I patted the side of his truck. "Thanks for stopping by, Boz. We've got work to do."

As he disappeared down the lane, Judy stood with fists on hips. "These potties of yours are about to fly all across the bay?"

"Let's be clear," I said. "They're *your* potties now. But don't worry. They float."

"Not if I don't sign this contract agreeing that everything you promised is on the property. Those are *your* potties, White Judy." She took her keys out of her purse. "I need to get off this island before the storm hits." She reached into her bag and threw the final contract at me, papers fluttering to the ground.

"Okay, okay, okay," I said, picking up the papers. "It won't take me long to round up eleven potties. Why don't you come along so you can learn how to do it?"

Back in her car, Judy poked at her phone. *Could she yank her deposit back out of my account?* I stood like a cow in front of her Lexus emblem while she slapped the dash and yelled for me to move. Finally, she got back out, removing her blazer. "Listen, I'm not going to ruin my suit over this. How long will it take?"

"No more than an hour. Then you can sign the papers, drop me at the airport, and get out of Hurricane Ivan's path."

She plucked out her gold knot earrings and dropped them in her purse. I was glad when she asked to use the bathroom before we left so she wouldn't see me push-starting the truck. When she returned, she had removed all her jewelry, including her watch, and rolled up her sleeves.

Our first stop was a house lift near the lighthouse. I grabbed the hand truck and flipped down the trailer gate. With two decades of experience, I made it look easy to roll two potties onto the trailer and strap them down tight.

"Why are they lifting this house," Judy asked. "Does it flood often around here?"

I wasn't going to tell her that scientists predicted half of Mobjack would be under water in a decade if sea levels continued to rise.

"Nah, the come-heres like a better view."

While I drove, Judy bit her lip as she thumbed away on her phone. "That man wasn't kidding. This storm is hitting the Outer Banks now. We need to get out of here."

Our next stop was a kitchen remodel near the courthouse. We hadn't seen any other vehicles since we set out, which was making me nervous. Boz was right—if I didn't round up these last potties, they would fly, and Judy would never sign the papers and wire the rest of my money.

"Where is everyone?" Judy asked. "Have they all left?"

"Nah. Only the come-heres evacuate. Everyone else is home, tying down their porch furniture."

"But the evacuation coordinator said it was mandatory."

"He has to say that, but we make our own call in these situations. Didn't you say you have people here?"

"No. I said my people were *from* here." She turned to face me. "They left in 1915 after my great-grandfather was almost lynched."

"Better check your facts." I turned on my country music. "Mobjack has never been a place like *that*."

"I *have* checked my facts, thank you very much." She turned the radio down. "In 1915, over a hundred and fifty Black families lived on Wynn's Island, owning and operating thriving businesses. How many live there now?"

"Oh, I dunno. Too many to count, I'd say."

I hopped out of the cab to collect my sixth potty. We were going to have to return to the island to unload these before picking up the next bunch because my trailer only held six.

"You can't count, White Judy," she hollered out of the passenger window. "There are none, zero, zip."

When I returned, she picked up where she left off. "The official story is that the Black families left to find better work, but the fact is, they were prosperous merchants and shipbuilders who owned a lot of land. My great-grandfather was almost lynched for supposedly starting a bar fight. He only survived that night because the sheriff put him in jail."

"Yeah, and who do you think put him in a rowboat and paddled him to safety on the mainland?" I blurted. "My people did. *Before* Wynn's Island had a swing bridge."

"So, you *do* know what I'm talking about." She leaned forward.

"Everyone does, but nobody's like that anymore." I was driving so fast over the swing bridge, I feared my potties might come loose.

When we arrived back at the house, I unloaded as fast as I could.

"The land this house is on," she pointed at her feet, "was once owned by my family. I looked up the court records online, and they show that after my great-grandfather was forced to flee for his life, Whites from the mainland bought all the Black properties and businesses on Wynn's Island for pennies on the dollar."

I nudged her back into the truck so we could pick up the five remaining potties.

"That was a hundred years ago," I shouted over the wind, careening onto the big road. "People in Mobjack are different now."

When I reached the swing bridge, the stoplight was flashing yellow and the wishbone gate was on its way down. I slammed the brakes. Judy braced her arms against the dash as my back end fishtailed and the smell of burnt rubber from my bald tires wafted into the cab.

"What the hell?" I shrieked. "We don't have time for this."

I got out of the truck and waved at Fletch, the bridge tender. He slid open his little window and hollered into the wind. "Coast Guard requires...bridge closed...duration of the storm."

"But I'll miss my flight," I yelled back.

He shook his head and closed his window.

I kicked a mound of oyster shells again and again until one of my Crocs flew into the water. The channel foamed and surged over the riprap while dark purple storm clouds hurtled toward us. My hair splayed and whipped my face in the swirling wind.

Judy got out of the truck, turning sideways to protect herself from flying debris. "White Judy—get in the truck." She put me in the passenger seat and then, with all her might, pushed the truck to start as I watched my Croc circle in an eddy just out of reach.

Back at the house, tree branches cracked, and fall leaves spun into mini-tornadoes. We hurried inside.

Pointing me to the couch, she stabbed at the TV remote. The cable dish had fallen off the roof a long time ago, and I never replaced it. "Doesn't *anything* in this place work?"

"Why," I changed the topic, "would you buy a house and a business without driving two hours to see it first? Who does that?"

"*Black* people do *that* when we suspect White people won't give us a fair deal. White people swindled us out of our land on Wynn's Island and stole our businesses in the first place."

That's when the power cut out.

After we both cursed and blamed the other for the situation, she groped her way to the garage to find the generator I showed her earlier. I heard her hit it with the heel of her shoe and thought, *Now she's catching on.* Joining her in the dark, I tried to show her the proper technique, but it still wouldn't start.

Swing Bridge

I'd emptied the house of everything but furniture, finishing my last frozen meal this morning. Now we had no food or even water since the well pump ran on electricity.

"Isn't there someone on this island we can stay with? You said the locals don't evacuate."

I started making calls, first to my ex-husband, then to the restaurant at the marina, then to the pastor of the church. Everyone was shocked that I hadn't evacuated and told me there was nothing they could do to help now that the storm was bearing down. The pastor advised me to give my phone a rest, to hold some charge so I could call for help in the morning.

Judy said she had some Pepsis and diet bars in her car. That reminded me. We needed to move the vehicles to higher ground in case of flooding.

A crack of lightning lit everything for a terrifying second, followed by the deafening sound of something heavy falling through the roof. No doubt, that dead oak I didn't want to pay to have removed. Scared to death, we fumbled in the dark toward her car, me with only one shoe. She jammed the key in the ignition, and we sped out of the woods, abandoning my truck and everything else.

I directed her to the old cemetery in the middle of the island. We parked in a wide, open area between overgrown Black gravestones on her side, and neatly groomed White ones on mine. We both checked our phones—no service.

"Ya know," she said, "our insurance companies are going to have fun deciding who has to pay for that roof."

I perked up. *Was she still considering signing the contract?*

"Don't you get it?" She reached for her purse. "I want the *land* my family owned a century ago. I don't give a damn about your potties.

110

If you collect the rest from wherever they end up after this storm, I'll sign the contract. I don't want any legal responsibility for your mess." She turned on the overhead light, flipped down the vanity mirror, and replaced her gold knot earrings. "Just once," she sighed, "I'd like to meet a White person who isn't afraid to tell a Black person the truth."

I switched off the overhead light so she wouldn't see my victory face. We sat in the dark, listening to the storm rage.

"You can take a nap," I said. "It's gonna be a long night."

"How can I sleep in a car with a racist and everything outside flying? This car might be picked up and thrown across the island."

"This is the safest place to ride it out. Let's take turns keeping watch."

Her wish for truthfulness hung in the car, making me feel guilty.

I drew in a deep breath and exhaled an apology. "I'm sorry I lied to you, but I *need* to get off this island. There are *no* single men in Mobjack. When one finally sailed up, practically to my door, I was trapped here by my home and business. They're all I own. I built Judy's Toilet Rentals from scratch after my grandparents died and left me the house. Now that my son is grown, I can't stand one more humid summer on a toilet rental farm. I would've lied to *anybody* to make the sale go through, so don't take it personally."

Everything outside fell quiet as the eye of the storm passed over the island. Black Judy inhaled a long, gravelly snore.

"Are you even listening to me?"

Her breathing seemed to stop altogether before a new snore formed.

"My son says I'm racist too, but I don't mean any harm."

I guess she had good reason to be annoyed with me. Pop-Pop always said our family got the land cheap, but never said why. That idea made me feel bad for the Black Tolivers. I began to admire Judy for her bravery, but I didn't say it out loud. She might have been pretending to be asleep.

I leaned over the console to turn on the radio. Finding a scratchy local news broadcast, I reached into the back seat to grope for the diet bars. Eating one after another, I pictured myself in my new bathing suit, lying on the deck of Jimmy's boat.

Surrounded by empty wrappers, I sank into the buttery leather seat, wondering if Judy would still drive me to the airport.

The Kittiwake

WHEN THE PANDEMIC STRUCK, the office at Whitman's Marina shuttered overnight, marooning the liveaboards on Sandy Bottom Creek like a lost colony. Onboard the Kittiwake, Fran cradled her partner's wasted body, pleading with Jackie to come back, to tell her how to handle this. As the afternoon passed, light rippled across the low ceiling, moving from the bow hatch to the bilge pump. Fran's shallow breathing gradually deepened. At sunset, she kissed Jackie's forehead and rose to call her daughter.

The still water surrounding Whitman's Marina gleamed metallic, like a bead of mercury. After Fran traipsed across the boatyard to find a working pay phone, mud clung to the soles of her red Top-Siders. She removed her shoes and placed them in a bin on the Kittiwake's portside deck. Inside, she leaned against the pilothouse door until the lock mechanism clicked, then tugged once more at the stubborn half-inch gap between the curtains.

"Alice is on her way," Fran said, lifting her voice toward Jackie's body in the sleeping quarters. She no longer expected a response, but she wasn't ready to end their twenty-year-long conversation. "Alice says it's a twelve-hour drive from Quebec to Virginia, so she should arrive by daybreak. I begged her not to drive at night. 'What's your rush,' I said, 'Jackie's already dead.' But she never listens to me."

Stepping down a wooden ladder into the galley, Fran clicked on the propane burner to heat water. "Want some of my tea, Jackie? We're out of your chai." Fran began to hum a tune by the McGarrigle sisters that reminded her of a time before she and Jackie met.

"I know you and Alice don't always see eye to eye. You're both so headstrong—but look how much she cares about you. She's driving all night for you." Fran chuckled, "Remember the time Alice's boys came aboard? You took us to that dive site with the sunken ship near Isle La Motte? You really are good with children, Jackie. You just need more patience."

The tea kettle whistled. Fran poured herself a cup of mandarin orange oolong. She sat at the dinette with her socks on the cushion and her knees folded like a grasshopper to keep warm. The thermostat in the pilothouse read seventy-eight degrees, but Fran was always cold.

"Alice says they still have two feet of snow on the ground up there. I told her she won't need her winter parka down here. The azaleas are starting to bloom."

That reminded Fran to throw away the dried-up daffodils and forsythia Lorraine had left on the dock beside the Kittiwake when she heard Jackie had COVID-19 symptoms two weeks ago. Fran had

removed the rubber band and newspaper wrapping from the stu
before placing the flowers in a mason jar on the dinette, setting aside
the newspaper to read later.

Lorraine kept the books at Whitman's Marina. Over the twenty
years that Fran and Jackie had lived on the Kittiwake, Lorraine was
Fran's only real friend besides Jackie. Fran looked forward to returning
to Whitman's each fall to resume their friendship until April, when
Jackie would begin preparations to sail back north to Lake Champlain
for the summer. When news of coronavirus first flooded the marine
radio waves, Jackie insisted the pandemic wouldn't make any difference to their daily lives. Never liking to admit she was wrong, Jackie
fumed when she saw how fast Lorraine closed the office and stopped
coming to the marina. Fran decided not to show Jackie the prayer card
for healing that Lorraine had taped to the flower wrapping. Jackie
needed her strength to fight the virus.

"Do you think the Americans will try to stop Alice from crossing
the border? If anyone can get through, it's Alice." Fran smiled. "My
pretty blond pit bull. She'll tell them her mother's partner died. Maybe
she should say 'stepparent' instead of 'mother's partner' to make it
sound more urgent, don't you think?" She leaned across the bench
toward Jackie's bunk.

"Alice will have to drive through New York to get down here, won't
she?" Having grown up in Quebec, Fran's knowledge of America's
overland geography was still poor. She tapped her chipped, red-painted
fingernail against a headline from the newspaper wrapping. "Says
here they're burying people in mass graves in New York City because
funeral directors are overwhelmed."

"Oh, no." Her eyes widened with panic. Squeezing them shut,
she tilted her head back and moaned, "Jackie, I'm so sorry. I didn't

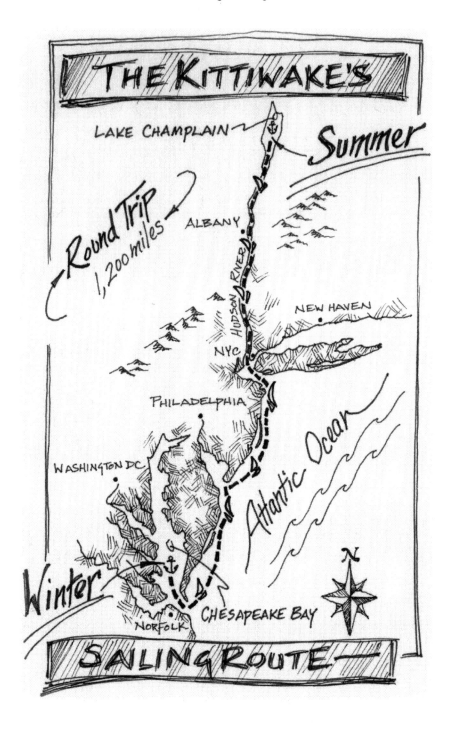

think. Alice will call the authorities." She smacked herself three times on the head, as if trying to get water out of her ear.

Fran reached across the helm for her cigarettes and lit one using the lighter that hung by a string over the nautical charts. In her attempt to get Jackie to eat something, she had forgotten to feed herself for the past few days. One of the liveaboards at Whitman's had suggested she try giving Jackie some of those calorie-filled milkshakes to build her strength, so she had taken the marina's beach bike into town and filled her backpack with cans of Ensure from the grocery store. All but one remained unopened next to the stove in the galley. Even though Jackie was too weak to eat, she had refused to go to the hospital. She had a deep distrust of doctors.

The marine radio in the pilothouse squawked with the Coast Guard performing evening drills. Jackie had always monitored channel sixteen for offshore distress calls and channel sixty-eight for local correspondence around Sandy Bottom Creek in case she could assist in an emergency. The marine radio broadcast was the only news she had cared about.

Fran scratched her head through her knitted beanie. She rarely took it off, even to sleep. She liked the way it contained her frizzy gray hair, which began to escape the longer she put off a haircut. Small and thin, she wore red leggings, which made her look even more like a kittiwake—the red-legged shore bird their boat was named for. They chose the name when they decided to follow the kittiwake's migration pattern, wintering in Virginia and summering on Lake Champlain between Vermont and Canada.

When Fran met Jackie at the Hertz rental car office in Burlington, Vermont, they were both middle-aged, wearing bright yellow customer service blazers. Fran smiled at Jackie from across the break room because Jackie seemed so uncomfortable. The short, spiky haircut and set jaw told Fran Jackie wasn't cut out for hospitality. Assigned to train her, Fran quickly realized Jackie wasn't trainable. Two weeks later, after the manager fired Jackie, Fran quit so they could sail away together on Jackie's boat.

Fran picked up the prayer for healing card from Lorraine and let her mind wander back to Saint-Jean-sur-Richelieu where she grew up. The nuns at her parochial school seemed so free from indecision that she briefly considered joining a convent before she got pregnant with Alice. Why hadn't she and Lorraine ever discussed religion, she wondered. *Had Lorraine secretly disapproved of her relationship with Jackie?*

"After I finish this cup of tea, Jackie, we'll clean you up. I'm going to put you in your Indigo Girls T-shirt and a fresh pair of jeans—just like you're headed to a womyn's music festival."

Struggling to get Jackie's bony legs into her Levi's, Fran worried Jackie's pants would slide off when someone came to move her because her body had shriveled so much in the past few days. Even the last notch on her belt wasn't tight enough to make a difference. Fran pulled out her sewing kit from under her berth and used cloth-cutting scissors to remove a pizza-slice section of denim. Then she forced a needle back and forth through the thick fabric until Jackie's faded jeans fit snugly on her hips.

After Fran sponged Jackie's face and neck, she noticed her fingernails needed clipping. Jackie's hair seemed to have grown more than usual since Fran had last cut it. Afraid of pulling too hard on Jackie's scalp, she gently trimmed and straightened her silver bangs.

"Hold still," she instructed, as she tweezed Jackie's chin.

Looking her over, something was missing. She had forgotten Jackie's glasses, which were folded in the cubby next to Mary Oliver's *Upstream*, the book of essays she was reading before she fell into a coma. Jackie had consulted Mary Oliver's poems throughout their relationship, so Fran tucked it under Jackie's arm. She wiped the lenses and placed Jackie's glasses on her face. *Shoes, or no shoes?* She knew Jackie always preferred to go barefoot, but Fran decided to pull socks over her feet anyway and wrestle on her L.L. Bean duck boots. As a final touch, Fran slipped Jackie's Swiss Army Knife and her "One Day at a Time" AA coin in her front pocket.

Satisfied that Jackie was ready for viewing, Fran picked up the VHF handset and tuned the radio to channel sixty-eight to transmit her message: Captain Jackie's time had come. Sandy Bottom Creek, where the river met the Chesapeake Bay, hosted some of Mobjack, Virginia's most expensive yachts alongside some of its most humble vessels. She invited the nocturnal liveaboards on the Creek to pay their last respects.

Placing the handset back in its cradle, she wondered if anyone would come, or if—like Lorraine—they would be afraid of catching the coronavirus. Without submitting to a test, Jackie had insisted she only had a seasonal flu. Fran never questioned Jackie. When the Kittiwake was underway, their mutual survival depended on a clear chain of command.

Fran peeked through the gap in the curtains to see if the "fellas," as Jackie referred to her rogue band of friends, would emerge from their floating shanties to answer her radio call. No longer seaworthy, most of their vessels were permanently moored, like a decaying reef. The liveaboards socialized by skittering around the creek in their dinghy boats at night after the day cruisers went home. Many nights, Fran fell asleep listening to Captain Jackie argue her philosophical and political views with a group of drunken fellas gathered at the end of the pier. Jackie was the only female in the group, except for a hooker named Wonder Woman.

Swing Bridge

To Fran's relief, the sound of outboard motors and the smell of exhaust began to pervade the creek as twenty or more skiffs converged on the Kittiwake.

"Permission to come aboard?" the first to arrive asked.

Fran sat in Jackie's captain's chair, swiveling to welcome them aboard, gesturing toward the sleeping quarters for viewing. Fran could smell that most of them had been drinking all day. She felt grateful to have met Jackie after she got sober. Jackie never swallowed a drop during their twenty years together. But because of her boozy past, she had always helped the fellas when they got into drunken scrapes.

The men stepped aboard gingerly, afraid to track any sort of disrespect into Fran's home. Soon their timidity gave way to shouting, each vying to tell Fran their story of how Captain Jackie had helped them out of a worse bind.

"I'll never forget how Cap'n Jackie towed me off that sandbar," a fella with kind eyes said. "I didn't know who else to call."

Another leaned in to confess, "Cap'n Jackie posted my bail—then she helped me apply for my Trump relief check to pay my court fees."

One with spider tattoos covering his neck gave Fran a wooden carving of a kittiwake he had whittled when he heard Jackie was sick.

Last to arrive were two young guys and a three-legged hound dog. They tied up their skiff in an empty slip and made their way over the wooden docks that crisscrossed the marina like lattice. Fran watched them approach as the men on board passed out Dixie cups and began toasting Captain Jackie with shots of Wild Turkey.

"Do you remember us, ma'am? We're the Foster brothers. I'm Willis and this is Hotdog. We owe our lives to Cap'n Jackie for the time our boat caught fire."

Fran recognized them, and their old dog sitting outside. Hotdog had taken his baseball cap off out of respect, revealing burn scars on the left side of his scalp, ear, and face.

"If you ever need *anything*, ma'am, you call us. Anything at all."

"Anything?" This was the first word Fran had spoken since her radio call.

Willis looked her deep in the eyes. "Me and Hotdog got you covered."

Everyone quieted to listen to a raspy-voiced fella with a guitar sing Jackie's favorite John Prine song. In the serenity of the moment, a simple solution came to Fran, as if Jackie herself had whispered in her ear. With a quickening pulse and courage rising from her abdomen, her gaze shifted from her folded hands to a white beacon in the harbor.

"One more song," she called before ushering the men off the Kittiwake—all but the Foster brothers. She had to hurry. Alice would be here soon.

* * *

Two hours later, when the tide peaked, Fran stood on the stern of the Kittiwake wrapped in the blanket she had crocheted for Jackie, watching the Foster brothers motor away in their skiff to fulfill her wish. She lost sight of their running lights when they cleared the jetty and turned hard to port toward deep water. After their watery trail stilled, she went back inside, pulled her knees to her chest, and removed her beanie. Tears traced the ruts of her tanned, leathery cheeks.

The clock in the pilothouse chimed four, reminding her that Alice would arrive soon. Jackie's belongings—her captain's log, her waders hanging on a hook, her bird-watching binoculars, her Christmas cactus—all seemed flat, like brushstrokes on canvas. Fran's tiny still-life of a home felt fragile. She drifted to sleep, satisfied she had not let Jackie down.

*   *   *

Static on the VHF radio roused Fran at daybreak as watermen on the Chesapeake motored down the creek to set their crab floats. She opened the curtains wide and squinted at the red sunrise over the bow. *Red sky at night, sailors delight; red sky in the morning, sailors take warning.* She stepped outside to loosen the spring lines.

Looking up, she saw Alice's white SUV, covered with splatter from the long drive, rolling into the marina's gravel parking area. When Alice got out of the car and stretched, Fran startled at the sight of her daughter in a surgical mask. Fran approached for a hug, but Alice backed away.

"Careful, Mom. You're contagious, and I can't afford to get sick. I need to keep a safe distance from you."

"Nonsense! I'm your mother. Come aboard and I'll make you a cup of coffee."

"Mom, I can't set foot on your boat or get anywhere near Jackie's body. Why don't you understand how contagious this virus is?"

"If it's so contagious, how come I don't have it? Jackie started feeling sick two weeks ago."

"I don't know. Maybe you're asymptomatic."

Alice had twisted her blond hair into a messy bun for the drive. She wore no makeup or jewelry. Her floppy McGill sweatshirt hung almost to her knees over leggings tucked into Uggs. Fran thought she looked prettier like this than when she wore a power suit and heels for her downtown lawyer job.

Alice took out her iPhone and told Siri to find the number for a funeral home near here. Fran listened to her daughter's side of the conversation.

"Not sure. Hang on—Mom, has anyone pronounced Jackie dead yet?"

"She's dead. There, I just did."

"No," Alice said, turning away from her mother. "No address either. The deceased lived on a boat at…" She glanced around until she saw faded lettering across the back of a metal storage facility. "The boat's at Whitman's Marina. Oh good, you know the place. You need her what? Oh, hang on." She took the phone from her mouth. "Mom, what's Jackie's Social Security number?"

Fran lit a cigarette and shook her head.

"It would be on your tax returns." Narrowing her eyes, she asked, "Wait, did you and Jackie even file taxes?"

Fran exhaled into the wind and squinted at the whitecaps building on the Bay.

"You would have needed her Social Security number to open a bank account or get a credit card. How do you pay for things, Mom?"

Fran glanced around the marina to see who might be listening. She didn't want others to know Jackie still had almost a thousand dollars aboard the Kittiwake. Fran's frugality made it possible for them to live on Jackie's Social Security check, which landed each month in Jackie's bank account in Vermont. Before heading south each fall, Jackie withdrew enough cash to make it through the winter.

The big bills were in a Ziploc bag in the engine room, behind the fuel filter. A smaller amount for everyday purchases was in the cigar box glued to the dashboard at the helm.

Alice finished her call and started taking pictures of the Kittiwake and Whitman's Marina as if documenting a crime scene. "The funeral director said he'd notify the County Coroner when we find Jackie's Social Security number. He's sending two guys over here to take Jackie's body to the Tidewater morgue where the medical examiner will pronounce her dead. They'll come as soon as they ensure they have the required PPE. Meantime, where's Jackie's will?"

Fran doubted Jackie had one. She climbed back onboard to see what she could find. After closing the door to the pilothouse, she popped open a porthole in the sleeping quarters to tell her daughter not to bother having the men from the funeral home come, but Alice wouldn't let her get a word in. If Jackie had written a will, she might have put it in the little safe next to the electrical panel. Fran didn't know the code, but she guessed Jackie would have used her sobriety date, 11-13. *Bingo.* The inside still smelled new. The manufacturer's warranty clung from a strip of red tape. The safe was empty except for a gun.

"Nothing in the safe," Fran called to Alice, closing it back up and scrambling the code. "She didn't leave a will, but I know what she wanted. A simple burial at sea."

"These aren't pirate times, Mom. You can't just throw her overboard. We have to notify the authorities and follow protocols. Since she died intestate, her estate will have to go through probate."

Fran filled her small watering can from the sink in the galley to revive Jackie's Christmas cactus, tenderly pinching off the dried flowers.

A boxy, black hearse approached like the shadow of a storm cloud in the parking area. Alice interrupted her list-making to greet it.

The Kittiwake

Fran reached into the back of the hanging closet for a large duffel bag. Then she retrieved her parka, winter gloves, and snow boots from a Rubbermaid bin under the stern deck.

Without asking permission for the men in hazmat suits to come aboard, Alice ushered them onto the Kittiwake. Fran began to object, but they pushed by, tracking clumps of mud from their boots. She shook her head and continued stuffing her winter clothing into her duffel while the men bulldozed their way back to the sleeping quarters. After a moment, the first one returned. Addressing Alice on the dock, he asked through his respirator, "Where's the body?"

"Mom, what's he talking about?" Alice used her prosecutor's tone. "Where's the body?"

"I told you," Fran said. "Jackie wanted a water burial."

The VHF radio squawked with the Coast Guard performing morning drills. One of the men from the funeral home held out his gloved hand to help Fran off the boat. She handed him her duffel bag instead.

Reentering the pilothouse, Fran knew she had no legal claim to Jackie's boat or bank account. She tugged at the curtains once more and stowed the last of the loose items before locking the door and lowering the Kittiwake's tattered pride flag to half-mast.

Alice consulted privately with the men for about twenty minutes in the parking area. When she returned to her SUV, Fran was sitting in the passenger seat with her shoes off and knees folded to her chest.

"You need to wear this mask and sit *all the way* in the back, Mom. There isn't enough hand sanitizer in the world…"

"Aye aye," Fran said to her new captain. She picked up Jackie's Christmas cactus and climbed over the console and the first row of seats with surprising agility for her age. Bending the wire in the surgical mask to the contours of her face, she said, "Turn up the heat please."

Gravesend

I WOULD HAVE GIVEN anything to trade lives with my older sister, Maddy. Our house had pictures of her everywhere. Ballet recitals. Cheer. Prom. The only ones of me were from when I was a toddler, when Mom could dress me like a boy. Like I would ever go *fishing* or wear *overalls*. I especially hated the one of me wearing a flannel shirt, sitting on a tractor. Maddy got credit for the good things I did, and I got in trouble for the bad things she did. Like this trip to London. I wrote the essay for her that won the contest to play Pocahontas in the BBC's tourism video, but Mom told everyone Maddy won because her Zoom interview dazzled the producer.

Swing Bridge

One of the ladies from Mom's Divorce Support Group gave us a ride to the airport. After we cleared security Mom pointed to Maddy's Fitbit, suggesting she get some extra steps before our flight to London. Maddy wasn't overweight but she'd promised the director she would shed ten pounds for the camera. She snarled, then set off.

Mom and I made our way to the Sky Club lounge, where we found a table next to the free snacks. Mom scanned the lounge through swollen eyelids for someone to talk to besides me. I kept telling her she was having an allergic reaction to her new liquid lash extensions. Tiny blisters were forming around her lash lines, but she refused to take makeup advice from her fourteen-year-old son.

"Fine," I said. "I'm going to the duty-free shop to sample the perfume testers."

Mom snapped and pointed at my seat. My brand-new passport had fallen out of the pocket of my phat pants.

"You mean cologne, Julian. Perfume is for women." She tucked my passport in her purse. "I'd rather you stay here with me. We don't have long before we'll need to go to the gate."

"I'll have a rum and Coke," Mom said to the waitress as she reapplied her vampy purple lipstick. Clearing her throat loudly, she caught the eye of a businessman two tables over. "I hope I'm not bothering you, but," she covered her face in mock distress, "this is our first time flying."

Pulling his leather cube chair to our table, he responded in a foreign accent, "I can assure you this is nothing to be afraid of."

I swiveled away to look out the giant windows framing the runway. This was not our first time flying. We flew to Texas every year to see Dad's side of the family, and we had flown twice to Orlando during Mom's breast cancer scare. It drove me crazy how Mom lied all the time.

"I mean, do I look like a terrorist to you?" She launched into a made-up story about how airport security had confiscated her shampoo and Swiss Army Knife.

He asked what the special occasion was for our first flight. To my surprise, Mom told the truth.

"My daughter, Maddy, won an essay contest to play Pocahontas in a BBC tourism video promoting travel to Gravesend, England. That's where Pocahontas died after John Rolfe took her to London to meet the king and queen. The BBC is paying for us to fly *premier* class."

The dude turned to me. "Congratulations! That's very exciting."

"Oh, no." Mom flushed. "This is my *son,* Julian. His long hair confuses everyone. The British Tourism Board offered to pay for the whole family to come. My ex-husband was even invited but he had to work. He's an engineer at NASA."

I swung around to give her the stink eye. Dad was a proud tugboat captain.

"We live in a small town on the Chesapeake Bay. Ever heard of Mobjack?"

Shaking his head, the dude finished his drink in one gulp and ordered another.

"It's in Tidewater Virginia," Mom continued, "where Pocahontas herself was born. You must have heard about the recent discovery of Werowocomoco? Fifty acres excavated along the York River? It was all over the news when they announced it's going to be a *national* park."

"We don't know about this in Estonia."

"You haven't seen the Disney Pocahontas movie? Werowocomoco is the site where Chief Powhatan met John Smith, and Pocahontas supposedly convinced her father to spare his life."

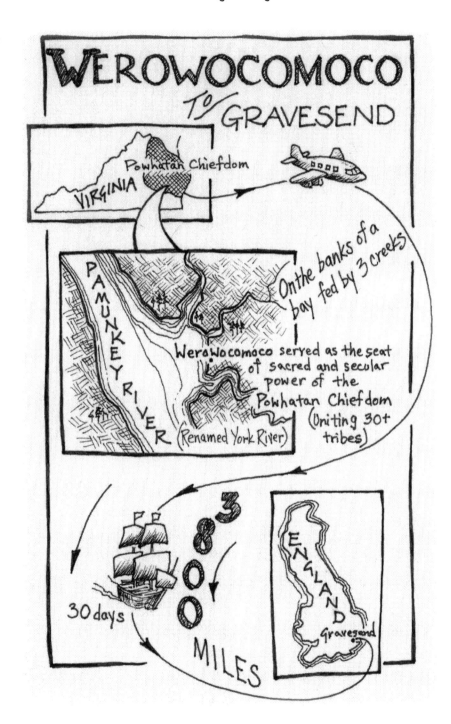

"*Supposedly* is right." I hopped in my seat. "Pocahontas was only ten. She wouldn't have been allowed to attend such an important ceremony."

"I was *trying* to tell the gentleman where we're from, Julian. Not reeducate him on early American history." She stage-whispered, "This precocious attitude is what I get for homeschooling him. He was bullied at school. We had no choice."

He waved away her apologies. "So the girl didn't save the man's life?"

"Couldn't have," I continued. "Pocahontas has been exploited for centuries, first to justify British colonization and now to promote tourism."

The dude reached for the nut bowl, arching an eyebrow. Mom looked at her watch.

"Only the Powhatans tell her *true* story. In the movie, Pocahontas is a hero who saves John Smith's life, but in real life she was kidnapped and sexually assaulted. The English held her for ransom, then forced her to convert to Christianity so they could parade her around London as a symbol of how they were *taming* the new world."

"Oh, snap. We're boarding." Mom stood up, dusting white cheddar from her sweater.

We hurried down the long corridor, jumping on and off moving sidewalks until we made it to our gate.

"She must already be on the plane," Mom said, stretching on tiptoes to see down the jetway. When we got to our premier-class seats, no Maddy. I shot her a text in all caps while Mom jabbed at buttons overhead, trying to call the flight attendant. I pulled her hand down and pressed the icon on her screen. When he appeared, she begged him to hold the plane for Maddy.

Swing Bridge

"We've had a sudden death in the family," Mom lied. "It's critical that she attend the funeral." She was extra convincing because her eyes were almost swollen shut now, like she had been crying for days.

As the plane pushed away from the gate, Mom went full monkey, throwing blankets and pillows. Other passengers told her how sorry they were, something would work out. I helped her wipe the mascara from her eyelids, daubing gently.

A few minutes later the aircraft returned to the gate. The heavy metal door reopened and Maddy slunk onboard. Everyone cheered and clapped.

*   *   *

As we descended into Heathrow the next morning, our plane tumbled through a bottomless cloud streaked with lightning. With each stomach-dropping bump, bags fell from the overhead bins. Mom started praying. Lying to God, I figured, about how we'd go back to church if the plane landed safely. Maddy slept through it all like a Disney princess.

I chewed my cuticles, scared of dying before I ever fell in love. To soothe myself I traveled to my happy place—the Reservation next to our house. I grew up playing along the banks of the river where Pocahontas came of age. Our favorite game was war between the Powhatans and the English. In our version the Powhatans forced the English into submission every time. I always won the high honor of playing Pocahontas because Chief Clear Water said I carried her spirit. Nobody cared that I was White, or a boy. Spirit was what mattered.

With a terrible thud the plane slammed onto the runway. Oxygen masks dropped from above. But we had landed on the ground, alive. A roar of applause filled the cabin.

Gravesend

After we cleared customs an old lady with short, white hair met us, holding a homemade sign: *Little Family*. Wearing sneakers and a track suit, she introduced herself as the mayor of Gravesend for thirty years.

First thing, she wanted a photo of herself with Maddy for the *Gravesend Gazette*. Raking her fingernails through her baby-like bangs, she handed me her phone. Instead of saying "cheese," she chirped, "Sex on a Wednesday," making us all laugh. Even jet-lagged with no makeup, Maddy looked great with her head tilted toward the mayor, teeth gleaming like a celebrity.

Outside it poured. "Sorry, I only have two umbrellas," the mayor said, handing one to Mom and the other to Maddy. Her car had a tiny back seat trashed with old flyers and used coffee cups. The boot only held one of our bags. Maddy sat up front while Mom and I sardined into the backseat with the rest of our luggage. On the highway the mayor launched into an infomercial on the history of Gravesend, how Londoners used to travel by paddle steamer down the Thames for the day.

"To see where Pocahontas died?" I asked.

"No, no, the excursionists were on holiday. Pocahontas was all but forgotten in Gravesend until the Americans took an interest. For centuries Gravesend was the last port of call for vessels heading from London to the wider world."

I thrust my face between the front seats. "According to Mattaponi oral tradition, John Rolfe poisoned her right after leaving London to return to Virginia. He stopped in Gravesend to offload her body."

"Rumors. We have *written* evidence that she contracted a fatal case of tuberculosis weeks prior to their departure."

"*Oral* evidence isn't rum—"

Mom gouged her thumb into my side. "Do you expect this rain to let up soon? I hope it won't interfere with filming."

Swing Bridge

I tuned out, lulled by the back windshield wiper, my face mashed against Maddy's backpack. When we pulled in front of the Rebecca Rolfe House, I perked up and whispered to Mom, "Looks like they still refer to Pocahontas by her hostage name."

"Blimey, it's raining sideways," the mayor said, trying to hold an umbrella over Maddy like she was royalty.

Mom directed me to take the stairs while she and Maddy rode the tiny elevator with our bags to our third-floor suite—two bedrooms adjoining a living room. Maddy and Mom each took a bedroom, and I got the pullout couch. "Hey, look." I snatched a note from the mirror. "The BBC film crew is staying in our hotel. The director wants to meet downstairs in the pub after we settle in."

"After that hellish flight I could use a drink," Mom said, wiping her tender eyelids with a washcloth.

Downstairs we stood in the doorway of the dimly lit pub. The director rose from his wingback chair, his gaze resting a second too long on Maddy's hips and thighs. Trying to recover his manners, he stammered, "Oh, I just—"

"You didn't expect her to be so tall." Mom saved him.

Meantime Maddy and I were checking out the English boy who had won the essay contest to play John Rolfe.

* * *

We hung out with John Rolfe and the film crew until after dinner, when Mom made me leave the pub with her, saying Maddy could stay for another hour. Back in the suite Mom zombie-crashed on top of her bed, fully clothed, one heel discarded in the living room and the other near her bed.

Gravesend

I rescued Mom's liquid lash extensions from the trash and used liner to apply King Tut eyes. Wearing earbuds, I practiced my dance moves in her heels, imagining John Rolfe's flirty reaction. When I heard Maddy struggling to open the door with her skeleton key at 2 a.m., I kicked off Mom's heels and faked sleep.

The next morning, no matter how hard Mom tried to wake her, Maddy could barely sit up. A member of the crew knocked on our door. I shot across the room to answer it, receiving two costume bags and a silk wig case. I desperately wanted to inspect them, but Mom said we were late for breakfast. On our way out Maddy slumped over again, snoring.

Downstairs Mom told the waitress, "Just coffee," while I ordered a pile of fried eggs, sausages, bacon, tomatoes, mushrooms, and fried bread.

The director pulled up a chair just as the waitress was placing my breakfast in front of me. "Julian," Mom said. "Try not to inhale your food like a skinny wolf."

"Bad news," the director said. "It's still bucketing down, so we'll have to rehearse inside St George's Church. Hate to lose a day. I'm on a tight budget with this one."

I couldn't wait to see the church where Pocahontas was buried, even though a fire had burned down the original, and the Brits were unable to identify her gravesite. According to oral testimony of the Powhatan entourage traveling with her, Pocahontas boarded the ship feeling fine

135

until John Rolfe invited her to lunch and poisoned her. Rolfe stopped in Gravesend to discard her body, then hurried back to Virginia to make his fortune in tobacco.

Maddy was late for rehearsal. The director asked me to stand in for her to read her lines. The script was pure propaganda, cutting between young Pocahontas frolicking in nature and a sad love scene on the banks of the Thames.

Maddy finally arrived, wearing the wrong costume. She had on the high-neck outfit and top hat over her wig, even though last night in the pub, the director had clearly said he wanted to rehearse the nature scenes first. To save time, he switched to the final love scene where John Rolfe carries Pocahontas off the boat, kissing her before she dies.

"John Rolfe," the director said, "you need to show more passion to emphasize how the English came to love and respect her as a true Christian princess."

John Rolfe was a murderer but, in this case, a mad good-looking one.

* * *

That night Mom managed to stay awake until nine. Maddy claimed she was turning in early too, but half an hour later she stood over me, wobbling on cheetah-print heels.

"Shhh," she said. "I'm going clubbing at the Pickle Factory with John Rolfe. Don't worry, we'll be back before it's time to film in the morning."

"I'll get my brolly!" I sprang vertically from my pullout couch.

"I'm sorry, Julian. I'd love to bring you, but you have to be at least sixteen to get in."

Deflated, I followed her to the elevator. "You know John Rolfe's gay, right?"

"Not possible." She adjusted her Spanx. "You saw how he kissed me during rehearsal."

"He was *acting*."

After Maddy left, I raided her room, dying to try on her costume and the wig made of human hair. I stayed up late adapting the script into a rap musical, tweaking the words to match the true story. My voice was starting to crack, but I read that drinking lots of water and doing voice exercises would keep it high and pure a little longer.

* * *

Mom shook me awake at 4:30 a.m., waving at me to get dressed while she dealt with a situation on the phone.

"Hello, Mayor? It's Mrs. Little. I'm so sorry to bother you at this hour. John Rolfe just called. My daughter's in an emergency room in East London with a fractured foot."

I guessed what happened. The amateur had never worn heels that high before.

"The Royal London Hospital," she said calmly. "They went clubbing at some place called the, the…"

"Pickle Factory," I supplied.

Mom shot me a look like she knew this was all my fault.

At the ER we found John Rolfe in the waiting room wearing a bomber jacket, his curly mop in a high razor fade, rubbing his gingerbread-brown eyes to stay awake. Maddy came out on crutches— one foot in a knee-high cast, the other still in cheetah print.

Silence hung in the car like heavy fog on the ride back to Gravesend. John Rolfe and I squished in the back seat on either side of Mom. By the way Maddy ignored him, I could tell she believed me now. As we drove east nobody mentioned the clear day dawning. Everyone had to be thinking the same thing: Maddy blew her chance to play Pocahontas.

When we reached the Rebecca Rolfe House, the mayor turned to Mom. "I'll wait here while you break the news to the director and pack your bags."

Mom climbed over me to open the door for Maddy, pushing me toward John Rolfe. He slid his hand along my thigh and rested it on my knee, making my root chakra jiggle like a bowl of marmalade.

In the lobby the director paced while the film crew sat on their equipment cases. "Let's go," he said. "We finally have the weather."

Then he saw Maddy's foot. "Oh, no. What happened?"

Mom nudged Maddy and John Rolfe toward him. "They'll explain." Turning to me, she said, "C'mon. Let's get packed."

Upstairs Mom slammed around the suite, rehearsing the lie she'd tell her Divorce Group friends. "Maddy was *killing it* as Pocahontas, but then John Rolfe tripped on a cobblestone and dropped her in the street."

When she started cramming Maddy's costumes back into their bag, I yelled, "Stop, Mom! I'll do it. You can't treat clothes that way. Look, you're tearing the deerskin apron. It's caught on the oyster shell necklace."

Mom dropped the dress on the floor, leaving me to hang it properly and get down to the lobby on my own with three suitcases.

When I stumbled off the elevator, the room fell silent. Everyone staring at me.

"What?" My eyes darted from Mom to Maddy to the Director.

Mom stepped forward and whispered, "The director wants *you* to play Pocahontas. I told him that's absurd. Let's go." She tugged my elbow.

"Yass!" I sprang into a pencil jump. "I was made for this role."

The director pleaded with Mom. "We've already lost so much

time. Production costs are way over budget. We must film today or this project will be scrapped."

Mom folded her arms at me. "Now you don't mind exploiting Pocahontas?"

"About that." I turned to the director. "I hope you don't mind—I've made a few changes to the script. It's more like a rap musical now."

He tilted his head, considering the idea.

Mom and I titlocked, like in Walmart when she refused to buy me belly beads and a crop top.

The director poked his head between us. "I hate to remind you, Mrs. Little, but you signed a contract. If Maddy fails to perform, you're responsible for your own travel costs."

Mom threw up her hands. "That settles it then. He has to do it."

"No." Risking everything in that moment, I wailed, "I won't play Pocahontas unless you *want* me to. I'm tired of the way you treat me. Everyone but you accepts my female spirit. I hate how you're always trying to change me."

She looked embarrassed, aware of everyone watching. "I'm doing what's best for *you*, Julian. That's my job as your mother. The world is a harsh place for people like you. I want you to fit in so you can be happy."

"I would be *happy*—" my voice cracked, "—if you would stop forcing me to be someone I'm not. You make up lies about everything, including who I am."

Her face puckered with self-pity as tears squeezed to the surface. She fished a package of Kleenex from her purse.

The director cut in. "I won't hold you to the contract, Mrs. Little, but can I tell you the truth?"

"Sure." She blew her nose.

Swing Bridge

"Your son would make a beautiful Pocahontas. He has grace, fine bone structure, and a photogenic presence that the camera will love."

Mom watched everyone's head nodding, including Maddy's. She took a step back to look at me, searching for what they saw. After inspecting my asymmetrical shag cut, she gave me a hug and surrendered. "I suppose he *is* beautiful."

The room blew up with cheers and clapping. John Rolfe caught my eye and licked his upper lip. I bit my lower one in response.

The director guided Mom into the pub. "No, of course it's not too early for a rum and Coke." Turning back toward me, he said, "Julian, we start filming in an hour. Wear the deerskin dress and be prepared to share your script ideas."

Mom had been group-shamed into saying the right thing, but it was a start. I couldn't wait to tell Chief Clear Water. She had always loved the real me, not the one wearing flannel on a tractor.

I pressed the lift button to ride to the third floor. Inside the small elevator I admired myself in the reflection of the brass doors. With shoulders back, eyebrows on fleek, and lifted chin, I held my phone high to the side, spun slowly to find a flawless angle, and exhaled through kiss lips. *Click*

Author Acknowledgements

At long last I get to publicly thank Kat Sharp—love of my life, ideal reader, partner in everything, and amazing illustrator—whose common love of "Mobjack" gave me the courage to write and share these stories. Without her faithful support, multiple talents, and dogged willingness to read draft after draft, this collection would not have come to life. Likewise, I couldn't have done it without the love and encouragement of two other champions, my mother Brent Nunnelley Goo, and daughter Allison Liya Hughes.

I began my creative writing journey five years ago in my early 50's by signing up for Amy Ritchie Johnson's fiction class at the Virginia Museum of Fine Arts' Studio School. There I met a wildly fun group of writers who remain part of my inner circle today—Mary Jo Mclaughlin, Vivian Lawry, Jer Long, Ed Chavez, & Heather Rutherford. They witnessed my first embarrassing stabs at fiction, encouraged me to continue, and showed me the importance of laughing at ourselves.

When the pandemic hit in 2020, I sought refuge in Randolph College's low-residency MFA program in creative writing, which turned out to be one of the most expansive experiences of my life. I'm grateful to Gary Dopp, Chris Gaumer, and Laura-Gray Street for founding such a challenging, diverse, and supportive program. I continue to draw inspiration from my brilliantly talented mentors—Julia Phillips, Clare Beams, Anjali Sachdeva, and Maurice Carlos Ruffin, who graciously allowed me to publish their words of encouragement on the back of this book. I'm also indebted to my classmates, some of whom make up the core of my current writing community, especially Sayuli Ayers, Anne Sirney, Angie Dribben, and Louise Freeman.

Vivian's Critique Group has served as base camp for my writing. I'm thankful for Vivian Lawry's wise counsel, the group's bi-weekly deadlines, and the members' heartfelt critique.

At a critical time in my writing, I deeply appreciated a week-long residency at the Rockvale Writers' Colony. In this beautiful mountain retreat, surrounded by other writers, this collection came together.

It goes without saying that I owe a huge debt of gratitude to everyone in "Mobjack" who collectively inspired these stories. Special thanks go out to my local beta readers for their early help and encouragement, especially Missy Whaley, bobbi hatton, Pam Doss, Bev Holmberg, Kay Van Dyke and Gary Barker. For lending their words of praise to the final manuscript, I'm grateful to Shawn Cosby, Pam Doss, Bill Johnson, Missy Whaley, Lori & Greg Dusenberry, Ned & Dia Lawless, bobbi hatton, Karen Holmberg, Christine Johnson, Kay Van Dyke, Jan Towne, Bette Dillehay, Ben Richardson, and Gary Barker.

Author Acknowledgements

Some dear friends went above and beyond to help with this project. Carol Cissel's editing skills helped shape early drafts. I'm so grateful to Julie Moos for copy-editing and proofreading the final manuscript. Cat McKenney provided insight and perspective all along the way, and her husband John Kenny supplied the perfect cover photo. How can I thank Angie Dribben or Monica McCormack enough? It's not easy to tell a writer-friend the truth, but they both had the courage. Huge thanks to Allen Lee, who helped me understand my own spiritual process regarding these stories, and how to convey it to the Richmond Friends Meeting.

Finally, for this book and everything else I'm proud of in my life, I'm indebted to the memory of Aaron Barlow (1951-2021), my best friend, mentor, and confidant for thirty-three years.

Illustrator Acknowledgements

I am grateful for the many good people who have shared in the creation of these illustrations.

Dr. Rob Atkinson, Wetland Scientist, gifted me with his dry humor, insight, and plausible theories. He and others, Elizabeth Pennisi, Science Journalist, Dr. Michael Meyer, Entomologist, and Zachary Bradford, Natural Heritage Steward, furnished key elements that helped me interpret complex topics.

Dave Brown and Thane Harpole, Directors of the Fairfield Foundation's Center for Center for Archaeology, Preservation and Education, have opened new pathways for investigating our cultural history in Tidewater Virginia. They supplied sensitive and current understandings of local history.

The Virginia Master Naturalists provided support and information specific to the Tidewater area. Tom and Susan Crockett contributed beautiful research photographs from their local birding outings.

Swing Bridge

The Wild Wonder Foundation, and Rebecca Rolnick's ReSTORY-ation, gave me access to a community of inspiring nature journalists and stewards.

Angie Dribben, Poet & Artist, lent me her sense of wonder, connections and deeper meaning, her thoughts sparkling with possibilities.

Tim Saternow, Watercolorist, brought both gravity and levity to this challenging process.

Karen Holmberg, Volcanologist, shared her wealth of connections, ideas, and experience.

bobbi hatton, President of the Mathews County Visitor and Information Center, gifted the Swing Bridge project with her invaluable energy and devotion.

Finally, thank you Cat McKenney, for pressing through brambles to find a mossy old grave, exploring abandoned farmhouses, and turning down that road we hadn't noticed until today. You and John Kenny have been loyal through and through. So many precious memories. Love you guys more than I can ever say.

About The Author

Originally from Washington, DC, Bronwyn Hughes has lived in Tidewater Virginia with her illustrator-spouse, Kat Sharp, for over twenty years. Leaving a foreign service career with the U.S. Agency for International Development, Bronwyn moved from Senegal to Mathews County with Kat to raise their adopted baby from China. Upon arrival, she plunged into her new community, retooling as a small-town CPA, founding the Mathews Film Society, and spearheading the mosaic mural project on Main Street. During the pandemic, she earned an MFA in creative writing from Randolph College. In her free time, Bronwyn enjoys boating on the many creeks and rivers feeding the Chesapeake Bay.

About The Illustrator

Kat Sharp is from Richmond, Virginia and holds a BFA from Virginia Commonwealth University. After moving to New York City, she developed a career creating scenery for theatre, opera and film. Her work often took her outside NYC to such places as the Santa Fe Opera, Hawaii Opera Theater, and a film set in Vienna, Austria. Turning to teaching, she served as head scenic artist for Yale Repertory Theatre and lead instructor for Cobalt Studios. Currently, she focuses on illustration, especially of the natural world, from her home in Tidewater Virginia. Her work blurs the boundaries between cultural narrative and nature journaling. An avid citizen scientist and Master Naturalist, she enjoys kayaking, birding, and oyster gardening on the Chesapeake Bay.

All proceeds from the sale of this book benefit the Mathews Outdoor club.

Founded in 2021, the Mathews Outdoor Club (501c3) is a nonprofit organization dedicated to powering outdoor activities and promoting sports tourism in Mathews County, Virginia.

MOCVA.NET

Made in the USA
Middletown, DE
04 June 2023

32037006R00099